WHAT WE LOSE

WHAT

A Novel

ZINZI CLEMMONS

VIKING

VIKING
An imprint of Penguin Random House LLC
375 Hudson Street
New York, New York 10014
penguin.com

Page 209 constitutes an extension of this copyright page.

ISBN: 9780735221710 (hardcover)
ISBN: 9780735221727 (e-book)

Printed in the United States of America
1 3 5 7 9 10 8 6 4 2

Set in Bembo Book MT Std
Designed by Cassandra Garruzzo

For my family: Mom, Dad, and Mark

&

André, for teaching me how to write love

I want to write rage but all that comes is sadness. We have been sad long enough to make this earth either weep or grow fertile. I am an anachronism, a sport, like the bee that was never meant to fly. Science said so. I am not supposed to exist. I carry death around in my body like a condemnation. But I do live. The bee flies. There must be some way to integrate death into living, neither ignoring it nor giving in to it.

—Audre Lorde, *The Cancer Journals*

African-American women now have about the same risk of getting breast cancer as white women. However, the risk of dying from breast cancer remains higher for African-American women. . . . In 2012, African-American women had a 42 percent higher rate of breast cancer mortality (death) than white women.

—Susan G. Komen organization

WHAT WE LOSE

PROLOGUE

My parents' bedroom is arranged exactly the same as it always was. The big mahogany dresser sits opposite the bed, the doily still in place on the vanity. My mother's little ring holders and perfume bottles still stand there. On top of all these old feminine relics, my father has set up his home office. His old IBM laptop sits atop the doily, a tangle of cords choking my mother's silver makeup tray. His books are scattered around the tables, his clothes draped carelessly over the antique wing chair that my mother found on a trip to Quebec.

In the kitchen, my father switches on a small flat-screen TV that he's installed on the wall opposite the stove. My mother never allowed TV in the kitchen, to encourage bonding during family dinners and focus during homework time. As a matter of fact, we never had more than one television while I was growing up—an old wood-paneled set that lived in the cold basement, carefully hidden from me and visitors in the main living areas of the house.

We order Chinese from the place around the corner, the same order that we've made for years: sesame chicken, vegetable fried rice, shrimp lo mein. As soon as they hear my father's voice on the line, they put in the order; he doesn't even have to ask for it. When he picks the order up, they ask after me. When my mother died, they started giving us extra sodas with our order, and he returns with two cans of pineapple soda, my favorite.

My father tells me that he's been organizing at work, now that he's the only black faculty member in the upper ranks of the administration.

I notice that he has started cutting his hair differently. It is shorter on the sides and disappearing in patches around the crown of his skull. He pulls himself up in his chair with noticeable effort. He had barely aged in the past twenty years, and suddenly, in the past year, he has inched closer to looking like his father, a stooped, lean, yellow-skinned man I've only seen in pictures.

"How have you been, Dad?" I say as we sit at the table.

The thought of losing my father lurks constantly in my mind now, shadowy, inexpressible, but bursting to the surface when, like now, I perceive the limits of his body. Something catches in my throat and I clench my jaw.

My father says that he has been keeping busy. He has been volunteering every month at the community garden on Christian Street, turning compost and watering kale.

"And I'm starting a petition to hire another black professor," he says, stabbing his glazed chicken with a fire I haven't seen in him in years.

He asks about Peter.

"I'm glad you've found someone you like," he says.

"Love, Dad," I say. "We're in love."

He pauses, stirring his noodles quizzically with his fork.

"Why aren't you eating?" he asks.

I stare at the food in front of me. It's the closest thing to comfort food since my mother has been gone. The unique flavor of her curries and stews buried, forever, with her. The sight of the food appeals to me, but the smell, suddenly, is noxious; the wisp of steam emanating from it, scorching.

"Are you all right?"

All of a sudden, I have the feeling that I am sinking. I feel the pressure of my skin holding in my organs and blood vessels and fluids; the tickle of every hair that covers it. The feeling is so disorienting and overwhelming that I can no longer hold my head up. I push my dinner away from me. I walk calmly but quickly to the powder room, lift the toilet seat, and throw up.

PART ONE

I was born as apartheid was dying. In South Africa, fervent national pride and multiculturalism were taking hold as the new national policy. I was born in America, my mother was born in Johannesburg, and my father in New York.

My mother's entire family still lives within twenty minutes of each other. They are middle- to upper-class coloureds—mixed race, not black. Although my mom involved herself in some of the political unrest (she proudly saved a newspaper clipping from 1970 that has a photograph prominently featuring a handwritten sign she made), my family was quiet and generally avoided the brunt of the conflict.

My father was raised in New York and went to college in Philadelphia. In the year after his graduation, he went on a trip volunteering in Botswana. My mother was there, partying with some of her militant friends. Ostensibly, they were there collecting literature to distribute back home.

"Your mother was inescapable," my father told me. Not that she was ravishing, or enchanting, but that he simply couldn't get away from her. "When I went back to Philadelphia, she called me. And she called me again. When I called her back, she asked if she could come to America to live with me."

My mother befriended people aggressively. She was extremely opinionated and often abrasive. I sometimes hated the rough manner in which she dealt with people. Her favorite words were four-lettered, and she liked to yell at waiters in restaurants and people in line at stores.

My mother's roots were deep and strong. Her relationships with others were resilient; she had friendships that persisted over decades, oceans, breakups. Her best friends were all former boyfriends.

Most of her friends (and she had many) spoke of her offending them shortly after they met. One story my mother told often was when one of her best friends threatened to commit suicide after her boyfriend left her. She went to my mother for comfort, and my mother slapped her across the face, as hard as she could. Her friend's face was bruised for a week. My mother used this story as an illustration of how to be a good friend.

She had close bonds with the other black nurses at her job, with whom she could affect a West Philly accent to match the best of them. And she had a coterie of South African expats from our area, as well as some from Washington, D.C., and Boston, whom she sometimes invited to our house for dinner or to watch a soccer game. They called our house at all hours and begged my mother for medical advice in Afrikaans or Zulu. Their child had a fever, or their mother-in-law was acting crazy again—was it dementia, or just moods? Many of them lacked green cards and insurance. My mother was the reliable center of their ad hoc community.

My father was a mathematics professor for many years before he was promoted to the head of the department at the college. He was flown around the country to give talks and make inflated speeches about their research. My mother migrated upward from nursing assistant to head nurse at the university hospital.

I have never personally been a victim of violence in South Africa. I remember a neighbor who was stabbed when I was little—the neighbor knocking on my grandmother's door late at night; the enamel bowl, with water turned pink and hazy, that my grandmother used to wash his wounds. My mother was the victim of a smash-and-grab in the hills around our vacation home. The assailant broke the car window and snatched her purse from her lap. She never drove alone again.

But most of what I experience is secondhand, from my family and the news. Together, the stories and pictures constitute a vision of death and carnage that is overwhelming, incongruous to the plainspoken beauty of the country. I see no evidence of the horror, which is what makes it terrifying to me.

This is the secret I have long held from my family: South Africa terrifies me. It always has. When I am there, I am often kept awake in bed at night, imagining which combination of failed locks, security doors, and alarms will allow a burglar inside, inviting disaster. I fear that we will be involved in one of the atrocities we learn of daily.

After apartheid, crime in South Africa has been insidious and seemingly limitless. Citizens live behind locked doors, security gates, electric fencing. The more money a family has, the more advanced the methods of protection. I have seen the progression of defense methods in the years I have been visiting. When I was younger, every house, if it was large enough, had a crown of barbed wire atop its high security wall. Since then, the barbed wire has been exchanged for electric fencing. Single fortifications for each property are no longer enough; now many streets and neighborhoods are blocked off with turnstiles and patrolled twenty-four hours a day by hired guards.

The security of my hometown in Pennsylvania was way past anything my South African family could imagine. The town was populated by stately old colonial mansions, most of them worth millions of dollars. When family members visited from South Africa, they would ask, *where are the security fences?* Our neighbor, an old widow with a stubborn streak, slept with the front door wide open through the night. *Is she mad?* my aunts and uncles would ask. She may have been, but in that town it barely raised an eyebrow.

In winter, the houses were adorned by twinkling Christmas lights. My relatives asked if they could take pictures on our neighbors' lawns. We spent hours driving around to find the brightest displays, in neighborhoods miles away from ours. They would never have done this at home, my relatives said, because people would steal the lights. Robbers would climb up on the fences and the roofs and cut them down, then sell them on the black market for the copper wiring.

In South Africa, there was little rhyme or reason to the tragedies of daily life, but there was social order of an old-world type and magnitude. I didn't respect her, my mother would often say, because I didn't speak to her like a child should. But I wasn't any ruder than my school friends, who treated their parents as older companions or siblings. This type of equality was at the root of my mother's feelings of insecurity. In South Africa, elders were treated with extreme dignity that, in my eyes, bordered on the comical. My cousins never addressed their parents with pronouns face-to-face. Instead, even my middle-aged aunts and uncles with grown children of their own referred to my grandfather as "Da" or "Daddy" instead of "you." Thus, a casual request turned into an awkward and foreign-sounding statement, as they were forced to say, "Can Daddy please pass the salt?" I could never imagine such a sentence falling from my American lips.

One of my school friends called both her parents by their first names. My mother found her so novel and strange that she actually liked her. She called this friend her favorite, with heavy sarcasm. Whenever I spoke my friend's name, my mother would chuckle and shake her head, as if delighted at the thought that this girl actually existed.

Fear of flying is most often an indirect combination of one or more other phobias related to air travel, such as claustrophobia (a fear of enclosed spaces), acrophobia (a fear of heights), or agoraphobia (especially the type that has to do with having a panic attack in a place you can't escape from). Flight anxiety can also be linked to one's feelings about the destination. It is a symptom rather than a disease, and different causes may spur anxiety in different individuals.

There are many Web sites offering courses or information that treat flight anxiety, many written by pilots or ex–air transportation professionals. One of the sites, promising a meditation-based approach to aerophobia, lists an example of destination-associated flight anxiety.

A woman in Maryland is in a long-distance relationship with a man in California. The relationship has recently turned bad, and the woman decides that on the next planned visit she is going to break up with the man. She has preexisting flight anxiety, but the anticipation of the breakup compounds her symptoms. She is unable to sleep for weeks before the trip, and dreams of the plane she is on falling out of the sky and crashing into the Rocky Mountains. Her anxiety is so severe that she almost decides she isn't well enough to make the flight, but on further consideration, she decides that the relationship needs to end. Breaking up wouldn't be right over the phone. So she takes the flight and is nervous the whole time, even though she takes a Xanax just before liftoff, as prescribed by her psychiatrist. She breaks up with the man, which turns out to be difficult but necessary, and notices that her anxiety is much less severe on the returning plane ride.

We were on our way to Johannesburg from Cape Town, where we had just switched planes for the two-hour flight. It was twilight. A rainstorm had been going for the past few hours and thunder was just beginning to rumble far off in the distance. We left the earth moments ago; the plane finished its ascent and was beginning to level off. We were starting to relax in our seats, ready for the flight attendants to return to the aisles with their drink carts. All of a sudden, the plane jumped into the air, as if an invisible hand had pushed us higher. We rocketed upward, our bodies whipped against our seat belts. People screamed. Two people fell into the aisle. One lay there groaning; the other, a young woman of about twenty, screamed, "Mama, Mama!"

Outside the windows, bright light flashed, and inside, the cabin was whitewashed for an instant.

My parents, sitting on either side of me, each grabbed one of my arms. I heard my mother start to pray.

Then the plane righted itself. The passengers around me slowly relaxed, first shakily fixing their hair, tightening their belts, murmuring. Then their voices returned to normal and, smiling at each other, they began pressing the buttons for the flight attendants. "Close call," I heard someone near me say with a sigh.

The pilot came on the loudspeaker to tell us we had been hit by lightning. Despite our fright, no damage had been done to the plane. The rest of the passengers, including my parents, all seemed to forget the incident after this, but I was frozen in my seat, terrified. My mother noticed and called for an attendant to bring me a glass of red wine. The alcohol soothed the circling thoughts of danger and fear, and soon I fell asleep, though something of this moment never left me.

Most of my family lives in or around Sandton, known as the richest square kilometer in Africa. It is a suburb of Johannesburg, home to luxury malls and complexes of mansions so heavily guarded you can't even see their street signs unless you're granted access. Sandton lies a forty-minute drive from some of the poorest townships in the country, where many of the gardeners, housekeepers, and security guards who tend these opulent homes and businesses live. This situation—the close proximity and daily interaction of the ever-stratifying classes—has led to the country's new postapartheid violence.

I have two aunts who live within the neighborhood limits, and an investment banker cousin who will move into one of the million-rand apartments in the grand Michelangelo Towers as soon as they are built. Our vacation home sits just minutes away from Sandton's busy commercial drag, in a quieter neighborhood that is on a level of wealth nearly indistinguishable for anyone not from the area.

Oscar Pistorius was born and raised here, and attended a primary school just down the hill from my family's vacation home. When I heard the details of the killing of his blonde model girlfriend, I found his explanation of the crime plausible. American news outlets made headlines out of his fascination with guns. He joked about arming himself when surprised by the sound of the washing machine. This does not shock me or strike me as out of the ordinary. All of my male family members own guns. My most hotheaded cousin sleeps with a loaded pistol under his pillow. (Miraculously, no fate similar to Oscar's has befallen him.) I can understand the sense of fear—waking in the night, seeing your bedroom window open, the evening air breezing through the curtains. I can understand reacting with the most force, because in South Africa, the worst outcome often happens. Rarely are you overestimating your own safety. It seems fully possible that he responded reflexively, especially given that he has no legs, and must have felt an ingrained vulnerability for years because of that fact.

But that same vulnerability might have produced an ego in Oscar that would propel him to dominate beautiful women, that would drive him to control a woman as desired and independent—as capable of leaving and being with another man—as Reeva Steenkamp. I chose to believe this story, of the athlete ruined by fame, instead of believing my worst thoughts and fears about my other home country.

From a blog post, "Some Observations on Race and Security in South Africa," January 6, 2015, by Mats Utas, a visitor to Durban from the Nordic Africa Institute

But how dangerous is it really? We try to investigate. Talking to taxi drivers is interesting. A black South African says that he would never walk around in downtown Durban late at night because of the immanent dangers.[1] He states that people are frequently robbed [during the] daytime or pickpocketed, but investigating further he has only once in his entire life been pickpocketed and never robbed. Nothing has been stolen from his home in one of the residential townships. An Indian taxi driver complains about the increased insecurity in the city, but he has never been robbed during the twenty years (!) he has run the taxi. Once his house was burglarized and the thief stole his wallet, phone and cigarettes—nothing more. His response was to raise the wall half a meter. The taxi agency he works for runs throughout the night, and although most of the company's drivers are Indians, the nighttime drivers are black, actually Nigerians: "they are much smarter at night". When we ask him if they are robbed, he simply says no.[2]

1 In this text I use the grossly simplified race and national labels in the same way as they are used locally.

2 I am neither diminishing incidents of crime in Durban nor arguing that people have no reasons to protect themselves. South Africa has a very high level of crime and I have also come across gruesome stories of violent crime. However in this text I am more interested in how insecurity cements racial categories. South Africa has roughly 16,000 homicides a year equaling about 30 per 100,000 inhabitants, roughly the same as Bahamas but well above Russia 10, US 5 and Sweden 1. Honduras with 90 homicides per 100,000 inhabitants is worst struck according to World Bank statistics.

Kevin Carter was the first professional photographer to document a brutal necklacing execution, in which a victim has a gasoline-soaked rubber tire placed around their neck, and the tire is lit on fire. His photo of a Sudanese child emaciated from famine, struggling to walk while a vulture gazes at her from the background, came to symbolize the desperation on the African continent in the 1990s. Carter, a white South African born to liberal parents, was drawn to the racial conflict going on in the black townships of Johannesburg. According to his friends, he empathized deeply with the plight of blacks under apartheid and experienced tremendous guilt for being a white South African. This guilt, combined with his constant exposure to the atrocities that were part of his job, were reportedly major factors that led him to abuse drugs.

In April 1994, Carter found out that his photograph of the Sudanese child had won the Pulitzer. A few days later, his best friend, photographer Ken Oosterbroek, was killed in the Thokoza township while documenting a violent conflict. Carter had left that scene earlier in the day, and after his friend's death, he agonized that he "should have taken the bullet" for him. The Pulitzer-winning photograph drew criticism from those who thought Carter should have done more to save the child, as well as from fellow journalists who found him inexperienced and undeserving of the honor.

In July of 1994, three months after his win, he committed suicide by running a plastic hose from his exhaust pipe to the passenger-side window of his truck. In his suicide note, he wrote:

"depressed . . . without phone . . . money for rent . . . money for child support . . . money for debts . . . money!!! . . . I am haunted by the vivid memories of killings & corpses & anger & pain . . . of starving or wounded children, of trigger-happy madmen, often police, of killer executioners . . . I have gone to join Ken if I am that lucky."

"Some Observations on Race and Security in South Africa," continued

On the other hand in the game of blame-throwing much negative is given to the Nigerians: they are amongst [the other ones] controlling the drugs trade in the Point area of Durban. When it comes to distrust it is all about categories of difference and appears and almost always in racialized terms. Indians don't trust the black South Africans, the white blames the black, but also the Indians, the black community distrust the whites. The only thing they appear to have in common is that they all distrust the Nigerians. Is that the basis to build new South African security upon?

To my cousins and me, American blacks were the epitome of American cool. Blacks were the stars of rap videos, big-name comedians, and actors with their own television shows and world tours. Notorious B.I.G., Puff Daddy, Janet Jackson. Martin Lawrence, Michael Jordan, Halle Berry, Denzel Washington. We worshipped them, and my cousins, especially, looked to the freedom that these stars represented as aspirational. It was a freedom synonymous with democracy, with political freedom—with America itself. It was rarefied, powerful.

But when I called myself black, my cousins looked at me askance. They are what is called coloured in South Africa—mixed race—and my father is light-skinned black. I looked just like my relatives, but calling myself black was wrong to them. Though American blacks were cool, South African blacks were ordinary, yet dangerous. It was something they didn't want to be.

American blacks were my precarious homeland—because of my light skin and foreign roots, I was never fully accepted by any race. Plus my family had money, and all the black kids in my town came from the poorer areas. I was friends with the kids who lived on my block and were in my honors classes—white kids. I was a strange in-betweener.

Yet my parents always spoke of a strong solidarity with black people in Africa. To call themselves something other than black was to take on the divisions of apartheid that grouped them according to skin tone and afforded them unequal privileges to keep them beholden to the state. They had been unfairly segregated, and it was their wish to live outside these divisions. That was something I absorbed, that never left me as the years went by. But when I expressed this desire outside the house, I was met with confusion and, at the worst, hostility.

At a party during my senior year of high school, when my friends and I were just beginning to drink beer and learn how to be ourselves in the company of these new factors—drunkenness, adulthood—I mentioned, as I often did (I fashioned myself as a politically engaged contrarian in my high school years), that I was the only black person at the party.

"But you're not, like, a *real* black person," a white girl named Anabel said to me, smiling, solicitation in her eyes. I felt ashamed, stunned. Uncomfortable, I said nothing, and after that day I never spoke to her again, indignant, but still unsure how to respond.

That the tragic aspects of American blacks' legacy are largely visible to the rest of the world is something I realized only later. I can quote our poverty rates, our mortality rates, black-on-black crime, and narrate the story of America's prison system, which churns black men in and out like assembly-line products.

My naïveté, my feeling of rejection, made my identification all the more strong. I only desired to belong, and I idealized this group as one does a storybook character or a superstar, or anything one doesn't know firsthand yet loves like an old friend.

Fuck the world, fuck my moms and my girl
My life is played out like a jheri curl, I'm ready to die

My mother cautioned that I would never have true relationships with darker-skinned women. These women would always be jealous of me, and their jealousy would always undermine our friendship. She told me to be careful if I ever went into the city, that the rough teenage ones would slash my face with a razor blade. When I fought with a friend, my mother would inquire about her complexion. If the friend was darker, she would nod her head, a look of "I told you so" on her brow.

I asked her how she could have such racist views of women. Weren't we all sisters?

"That's just how it is," she told me blankly.

My mother was a shade darker than me, with almond-shaped eyes and hair that was slightly coarse but straightened out easily with an iron. She was identifiably black, more than I am (I am often mistaken for Hispanic or Asian, sometimes Jewish), but categorically light-skinned. Sometimes people thought she was Spanish too, and dark enough that we often encountered the uncomfortable pause of a white woman in my hometown trying to discern our relationship: mother/daughter or hired help/charge.

My mother's views imbued my friendships with political

importance—if I could maintain a relationship with a darker-skinned woman, I would prove her wrong. And so I pursued these relationships with fervor.

I've often thought that being a light-skinned black woman is like being a well-dressed person who is also homeless. You may be able to pass in mainstream society, appearing acceptable to others, even desired. But in reality you have nowhere to rest, nowhere to feel safe. Even while you're out in public, feeling fine and free, inside you cannot shake the feeling of rootlessness. Others may even envy you, but this masks the fact that at night, there is nowhere safe for you, no place to call your own.

I see you looking at me. I know how you see me.

Aminah had been my best friend since elementary school. Her father was the administrator of continuing studies at the same college where my father taught. Together they were two of only five black faculty, causing them to form an immediate bond out of a shared, slightly traumatizing experience. Aminah and I went to swimming lessons and summer camp together as children; as teenagers we drifted in and out of each other's orbit at school, but our bond outside of that restrictive environment remained familial. Even if, on the surface, we seemed as dissimilar as possible, a calm, unshakable current of love always ran just underneath.

Aminah was a preternatural beauty. With long, jet black hair that sat in perfectly tame spiral curls, a slight frame, and clear mahogany skin, she fit in easily among the prettiest girls in school. She was mild mannered, though, quietly studious, and kind. She kept her stubborn streak expertly disguised. I always had a hard time maintaining any semblance of togetherness, from my hair to my clothes to my opinions that always seemed to make themselves known in the worst company at the worst possible moments. I had the feeling that I embarrassed Aminah, so I saved her the trial of having to reject me socially by leaving her alone at school.

It felt like a foregone conclusion when one of the boys in

our class fell in love with Aminah—one of the handsome boys from a good family who owned a lake house in one of the fancier vacation towns upstate. His name was Frank.

At first, there were rumors of tension because Aminah was black and Frank was not just white but a WASP, and his family had the type of standing that a black girlfriend could tarnish. At first, Aminah told me, Frank's family didn't invite her to the house, even though they had tea with his older brother Paul's girlfriend every Sunday afternoon.

The story that wasn't told was that Aminah's family members were just as wary of the union as Frank's, because even though they were now bourgeois, Aminah's father had been an activist and agitator back in the day, just like my parents, and they always hoped—assumed—that her looks and education meant she would have her pick of suitors, and that pick would be black, just like her.

Over time, these tensions soothed into the background, and Aminah and Frank became one of the envied couples at our high school, leaving room for all the other relationship tensions to resume their rightful place in the foreground.

I started listening to hard rock music with emotional lyrics, like my friends. We didn't have cable, so I spent hours at their houses after school, watching music videos on MTV and clearing their pantries of sugary snacks. My parents would never buy snacks, because they were too practical and too busy for anything more than three meals per day. "Snack" was a word that never entered their vocabulary. On weekends, I would take the commuter train into the city, sit in coffee shops, and smoke cigarettes while reading old paperbacks. I told my parents I was going to the central library branch downtown to study, which was partly true. I was studying for my grown-up life, the one I would have when I finally left their house.

Most of my friends were school nerds, but some of them also had piercings and tattoos. My friend Fiona had green hair. My mother liked her the least of my other friends, whom she called freaks. I told my mother, with practiced cool, not to be so dramatic. The few times I tried this, it made her boil over.

I never got up the courage to color my hair, but I often let it go curly and wild, refusing to straighten or restrain it from the natural way it fell on my head. I had the nerve to like my hair just the way it was. My mother called me untidy. "I don't know why you do this to yourself," she said, huffing and rolling her eyes. What she meant was, why do you do this to *me?* My self-expression obviously caused her pain. From the time I was five until high school, she dragged me to the hairdresser every two months to have my hair chemically straightened. She insisted, explicitly and implicitly, that straight hair was beautiful, and the kind she and I were born with—kinky, curly, that grew up and out instead of down—was ugly.

"That's what a pretty girl looks like," she told me when I came home from the hairdresser, my hair shining, my scalp in ravages. Only the thought that my mother would find me beautiful—the anticipation of her approval and the peace it would bring—would comfort me through the pain the next time I sat in the hairdresser's chair, to have it done to me all over again.

My high school boyfriend took me to prom in his beat-up hatchback Toyota. He was decidedly unspectacular—a C student who went on to a local university and dropped out after two years. He never left his small storefront apartment in our hometown. But he was handsome, with a strong, square jaw, sinewy arms, and smooth brown skin. He was polite, but with a bit of edge and tastes that ran toward the alternative, the slightly dark. We met in art class.

When I finished dressing, he was downstairs in the living room, talking to my father. They were like a teen movie come to life, my father with his chest out, protectiveness personified, and Jerome shrinking in his tuxedo, visibly nervous. "You look beautiful," Jerome said, sighing, when I came downstairs. In my head, I wondered at how my movie scene felt complete.

We never had sex, because I was too afraid and I wasn't in love with him. I was still young, and in my mind sex and love were inextricably linked. A few months into our relationship, I had my college acceptance in hand and began to dream about the handsome, worldly boys with whom I would be able to discuss literature and obscure music. I imagined how easy sex would be with them, how natural and adult it would feel, as opposed to what felt like a struggle between my desire and better judgment with Jerome.

But he made my parents happy in a way that I could never approximate on my own. When I was with him, a piece of me was in place, and I was a whole, acceptable human being to my mother. I was in some ways normal, and they could be happy for that. When Jerome and I broke up, it took me months to tell my parents. I would lie to them and tell them I was going to meet him when I was planning to see my girlfriends. After I revealed the split, my mother still asked about Jerome.

"He's leaving college," I would say.

"But he was so nice," my mom would say.

My college was four hours away by train, up in New England, one of the top places in the country. When I was accepted, no one was surprised—I was always known as a brain—but there was a renewed interest in me, both positive and negative. My teachers smiled at me in the hallways. A few from junior high made the mile-long trek to my high school to congratulate me. The white students who were disappointed in the admissions process—who ended up with their last pick, or somewhere low on their lists—were envious. Some started ignoring me, rolling their eyes, or snickering as I walked by. Two students went so far as to question me outright, calling me an affirmative action baby. It was always something besides that I was simply better than them. Anything but that I was better than them.

At college, at least I didn't have to deal with the problem of being exceptional. Everyone was exceptional in some way. Almost everyone was smart, and the ones who weren't were either amazing athletes or super rich—celebrities, aristocrats, or children of celebrities.

I flitted in and out of various groups—black kids, artsy kids, and, for a brief time, stoner kids. I never settled on one group, because I was preoccupied with what was going on in my family. Between that and my studies, I had no room for close friends.

Instead, I stayed close to Aminah, who was in New York studying literature at NYU. I was proud because I recognized for the first time her desire to be independent, the way she was drawn to a life outside of the one she seemed so comfortable leading in our hometown. It was most likely this choice that encouraged me to keep in touch with her after we had moved out of our parents' houses, that made me call and ask if I could sleep on her floor when I visited New York for a weekend concert, that led me to send e-mails and ask about her new life in the big city. That, in our first few years out of our respective nests, made us *friends,* not just sisters.

When Aminah left for NYU, Frank headed to Georgetown, and after never being apart for more than a night, they were five hours away from each other with little opportunity to visit. But somehow they seemed more blissfully in love than ever, and I realized that the divergence between our love lives—which had begun in high school—would be permanent.

I met Devonne in my first year at college. Fresh out of my monochrome hometown, where white was right and everything black was wrong, stupid, and ugly (I was a nonentity), I felt like meeting her was a coming-home. She was intelligent, fierce. She wore her hair in neat dreads. She wore horn-rimmed glasses, starched men's shirts, and designer loafers. She was sharp.

On the first day of our first-year orientation, the administration crammed our entire class into an auditorium, and when they asked if we had any questions, Devonne stood and recited a spoken-word poem, which she would later tell me she revised from one she had performed at slams in high school.

You don't see me when you pass me in the hallways,
Not the real me,
I'm just a black girl to you, with
Tough nails and
Tough voice.
I'm here.

There was a stunned silence, and then enthusiastic applause. My stomach lurched when she strode into my Africana Studies class the following Monday. I hung around after class, waiting for her to finish her conversation with the professor about Marcus Garvey. (*He was a world-class bigot. I won't celebrate him,* she said as our professor beamed at her.)

"I think you're right about Garvey," I said as she walked toward me. She smiled.

"Oh yeah?" she said. "Walk with me."

I told her that where I'd come from, my views and my skin made me a lonely little island. I told her I felt so happy to meet someone like her.

She just nodded along. "You know how many people told me that this week?" We stopped at a forked path on the college green. "I'm headed to the library. I'll catch you later."

I was sure that was the last conversation I would have with her, but the next day, I heard someone call my name from across the cafeteria. Devonne came bounding toward me, her dreads bouncing in the air, feet slightly splayed in her loafers.

She dropped a small paperback of C.L.R. James's *Minty Alley* on my tray.

"I brought this for you." She smiled, out of breath. "Where are you sitting?"

Our friendship burned fast and bright from there. Each day we would find each other in the library and spend hours in the stacks reading side by side. We took cigarette breaks together and marveled at the broody boys who kept us company outside, speculating on the love lives of the ones who offered us their lighters.

"I bet he's great in bed," Devonne would say, or, "SDS: Small Dick Syndrome. Did you see the way he fixed his hair constantly? Insecure."

"You're terrible," I'd reply, snickering.

At some point she noticed that they showed me more attention. One offered me a cigarette and not her; another spoke to us both, but kept his eyes on me.

"I didn't think you were interested," I'd say.

"Of course I'm not interested," she'd say.

Our friendship ended in the same place it started: in Africana Studies class. We all did oral presentations: Devonne spoke on Marcus Garvey, advancing her thesis that he should be treated in the same way as Hitler and Mussolini. It was bold but with noticeable gaps in thinking. I did a short presentation on Toni Cade Bambara, including an analysis of her role as the editor of notable anthologies of women's writing. After class, the professor approached me.

"Nice work," he said.

I looked around for Devonne, but she had already left. She wasn't in the hallway, or outside in the parking lot, where we normally had a cigarette after class. She wasn't in the library that day either.

When I saw her the next week, she told me that she'd slept with one of the boys we'd met outside the library who had looked at me. Though she'd feigned disinterest at first, she'd actually slept with him several times. She said she was in love.

"What a *jerk,*" I exclaimed.

Devonne stared at me, as if she was trying to decode something inside me.

"Yeah," she said slowly. She flicked her cigarette and turned briskly without her normal air kiss or sarcastic comment, and, for all intents and purposes, she was gone.

My first love was Dean, a philosophy student who played guitar with a band from the local art school on the weekends. He was half Spanish, with pouty pink lips and freckles, impossibly. We met at a concert downtown, and at the end of the night he stroked my face and asked me out for coffee the next week. We went, and halfway into my coffee, I felt myself sinking into the vinyl booth. I knew that whatever happened after this point would be irrevocably different. Before long I was spending whole weekends at his apartment downtown, mornings fucking on his dirty red sheets, afternoons sleepily plodding through our reading assignments. He gave me Sartre and Proust and the Velvet Underground and Bobby "Blue" Bland. He taught me how to blow smoke rings from his Marlboro Reds.

Early on I felt I had nothing to offer Dean except my body. He was a full person and I knew that I wasn't yet, that I was still growing, that he and our relationship were shunting me into being. I made myself available to him all the time, and it wasn't long before he'd used me all up, grown bored, decided he needed more.

I grew restless. I could barely focus in class, so I spent most of the day catching up on lessons, and then I stayed up through the night completing my assignments. I saw Dean at the library, smoking his Marlboros on the steps. At first he nodded hello to me with a manner that could be mistaken as warm, but the enthusiasm of those acknowledgments waned as the months went by, and eventually he didn't acknowledge me at all. He just let his eyes flit over me like I was a piece of stone in the library wall or some other student he hadn't known, like he hadn't once breathed, *I could love you, you know,* on my neck.

Then one day there was a girl—a thin girl whom I'd seen studying in the visual arts library. She had papery skin and a severe brown bob that framed cheekbones like snow-capped hills. She wore vintage dresses that I never could have squeezed into and smoked hand-rolled cigarettes. She looked designed to attract men like Dean, and it sunk in when I saw them together on the steps of the library that this was who he should be with, not me. It was never me.

I had no reference point for heartbreak. My insides felt emptied out, and there was no need for food, no need for sleep. At first I couldn't work—couldn't even focus enough to read a chapter without dissolving into tears. Later, work was all I could do to keep the swirling thoughts from coming in, the images of her in my spot on his bed, her eating oatmeal across from him at his kitchen table.

My parents grew into a very comfortable life in their middle age. After I left for college, they sold their house in the suburbs and bought a two-bedroom apartment in an upscale Philadelphia apartment complex designed by I. M. Pei in the 1960s. The three apartment towers overlook the Delaware River and decaying, bullet-ridden Camden, an aging beacon of the city's relative wealth.

They used the rest of the money from the sale to buy a vacation home outside Johannesburg and a VW Jetta that they kept in the garage. At least once a year, we flew to Johannesburg, and for at least two weeks, we stayed in the house, a modern stucco home with terra cotta tile on the roof. My father employed domestic workers to clean the windows and sweep the driveway while we were away, and to wash our laundry and mop the floors while we were there.

The vacation house sat atop a hill full of other posh, neatly kept homes to the northwest of the city. Within a half hour we could drive to the dusty three-room house my mother grew up in, where my grandfather still lived. The vacation house's huge picture windows looked off a cliff to the valley of Johannesburg below. From there, you could see the turquoise of the mansions that surrounded us, where my aunts and uncles lived, and, farther away, the red dirt and tin roofs of the townships clustered closely together. This was where my mother came from, and where my grandfather journeyed from to visit us, to spend a peaceful hour outside in his high socks and straw hat, sunning himself on the deck of our infinity pool.

My lover is kind. He is not quick to anger. He is measured and good-natured. Like a child, but not lacking in experience or knowledge. In the circuit of my life, he is the ground. He balances me, allows me to flow at an even rate.

He has red hair and he is not particularly broad or strong, like I had always imagined my one true love would be. My lover is definitely skinny. Try as he might to eat every carbohydrate and piece of red meat in his path, he can never put on any weight.

Yes, as much as I hate to admit it, I always imagined that I would have one true love, who in my later days would define me as much as my career or my personality. He would be a part of me, and we would come together and make another part. The picture wavered slightly over the years—at times I convinced myself that I would be okay alone, or with several partners; for some periods my husband was a wife. But it always came back to this picture: one partner, for the rest of my life.

My mother told me that a man's shoulders should be wider than yours, that he should be able to lift you easily. She didn't like skinny men.

Oftentimes I find myself, when we are fighting over the bills, or when he chews his food too loudly or laughs at the wrong time during a film, asking not whether I am happy, but whether my mother would approve of him.

His last name is one syllable—strong, uncomplicated. It reminds me of steel or stone. His red hair is thick in the front and downy and blond on the back of his neck. His face is smooth, like a baby's; he doesn't grow much facial hair, only a dusting of blond on his upper lip and a spot underneath the lower. He says it caused him a lot of shame in high school and college in combination with his lanky frame. The other boys called him Twiggy. Now he works out in the yard, lifting logs above his head, and runs for miles "to clear his head." No one in my family, going back to Africa in both directions, has ever run for any reason except self-preservation. He laughs at things like this and doesn't ask too many questions. He is interested in my background, in love with my skin, but not too in love. There is a casualness bred from familiarity that makes me at ease around him, that drew me to him in the first place.

When my lover and I fuck, we fuck with the fear of the world in us. We are fucking on the edge of a cliff. We are fucking death right in the ass, and death loves it. We are fucking our own deaths, and our mothers' deaths, and the deaths of our friends and the deaths of our rights.

One day, a sunny day at that, on one of my weekend trips to Portland, Oregon, we have sex for an entire day. We ignore the sun and stay in bed, and we eat and suck each other for twelve hours, and when we're done we order in Thai food and eat in bed. We fall asleep with dirty dishes on the floor.

At first I'm concerned about his landlady hearing us, but then I don't care. I am doped out like the worst of the dope addicts. I want to do this every day for the rest of my life, and I don't care if they find me ass-naked with my face in his lap when I'm dead.

I want to touch it.

I want

I'm touching it

Just there don't stop

Shit

Right there

Right thereRight there

Right thererightthererightthere

My parents were never openly affectionate with each other, or with me. I never saw them exchange more than a quick squeeze on the shoulders at the end of the day, a chaste peck on the cheek before the other left the house.

I learned about sex in my liberal primary school, which ensured we were given healthy doses of sex ed starting in kindergarten. We were given permission slips to have our guardians sign, tacit acknowledgment for my parents that their duty was being farmed out successfully. At home, even the word "sex" was censored out of conversation. It was as if it didn't exist in our house; sex was only a problem of the wild, tainted world outside.

But then one night, while I was in junior high, I heard my parents making love. I heard my mother panting loudly and eventually screaming, and my father grunting, in rhythm. I pulled my blanket over my head, terrified, shivering. I lay there for the rest of the night, my heart pumping, exhilarated and unable to sleep.

I didn't know what it meant at the time, but when I looked back years later, after experimenting and then making those sounds on my own, I felt something different than fear. Familiarity; and perhaps some satisfaction that my parents were, despite their coldness, in love.

In the weeks after my mother died, my sex drive was merciless. I was stuck in my bedroom while family and friends circulated in the apartment's outer rooms and hallways, barely able to leave my room, embarrassed for my eyes and nose that ran like faucets, my face blotched with red from wiping all the tears away. Aminah came and went, but there weren't distractions of the magnitude I needed to keep me from suffering.

I masturbated often, mostly at night, but sometimes in the day, while I could hear the voices of my parents' friends muffled through my bedroom door. I cycled through relief, then shame and horror, desperate for the release and powerless to stop the urge. I longed for the touch of someone else, but all I had was my hand. During the day, I envisioned my mother watching over me, and that comforted me. But when the urge inevitably came, I fought to banish the thought of her while pitifully jerking myself off in my childhood bed.

I work for a public health agency in Forest Hills, Queens a job that has systematically robbed me of my idealism since the day I started. With every day that goes by, every person who passes through our door, I banish further the possibility of anything ever truly changing for the better. I admitted this to my boss, an overweight middle-aged woman with dull red hair and three ex-husbands. She laughed at me. "So you're finally getting it, huh?" she said, and walked away from me, cackling all the way down the hall.

They sent me to a conference on HIV/AIDS pharmaceuticals in Oregon. I spent four boring days floating disinterestedly from presentation to presentation to hotel bar before I noticed Peter sitting across the table from me. He was attractive, with dark red hair and serious eyes, high cheekbones, and a slight curve to his shoulders that suggested muscles and experience. That night, after everyone had eaten dinner and retired to their rooms, he was sitting alone at a table in the bar, something dark and half-drunk in his glass. I asked to sit with him, tentatively. I was nervous that he would, for some reason, say no.

When he pulled out the chair for me, I noticed that he was reading a book: a new biography of Malcolm X. I had just read a review of the book and tried to impress him with my knowledge. He looked at me, interested but nonchalant, and asked if I had read the other biography released this year. "No," I had to admit, trying not to let my defeat show.

He told me he was thirty-three, seven years older than me. I repeated the Elijah Muhammad teaching my father had told me, that the ideal age for a woman should be one half the man's age, plus seven years. He smiled with one side of his mouth, and sat forward in his chair. I knew that I had him.

He told me that he had left a PhD program in literature a year ago. Global health was his plan B. It wasn't working out so well for him.

"I'm bored to death," he told me, dropping a heavy palm on the Malcolm X book. Instead of helping people in need he was managing a bunch of recent college grads. I admitted that I was bored too, and this time we both laughed.

This was the first time I actually saw his face, actually *saw* him. I imagined him stroking my hair, what it would feel like to look at him across my pillow. We talked excitedly, with no breaks in the conversation. I forgot to order a drink, and before I knew it, the time was 3:00 a.m.

We were assigned a site visit together on the other side of town. Afterward, he took me cruising through the streets of Portland. He showed me around downtown and Chinatown, and then took me to King, lined with hair salons and corner stores. He pointed out the shabby high school where his father worked as a principal. We ended up on the Columbia River near the entrance to the Hawthorne Bridge, and watched the expanse slowly lift into the air to allow a boat to pass underneath.

He parked in a lot and we sat on the hood, our arms braced over our winter coats. My mind was six moves ahead; I thought of my hands moving through his hair, what his breath smelled like up close.

He told me that he was moving the following week to a larger apartment with his girlfriend. The words came out coldly, and he didn't look at me afterward. We sat for a few more moments outside, and then I politely thanked him for the driving tour. We climbed back into his car and he drove me back to the hotel, where I barely slept that night, restless in my empty room. The next day, I got on a plane back to the East Coast, exhausted.

Afterward, I thought of him often, remembering the warm, excited feeling I felt for those hours I sat in the passenger's seat of his car. But I was angry that he had led me on, and I didn't reach out to him.

Eight months later, he e-mailed me, saying that he and his girlfriend had finally broken up. He invited me to Portland to stay with him for the weekend, saying he'd pay for the flight. I didn't hesitate much, but I also didn't tell anyone.

One afternoon in my senior year of high school, I came home to what I thought was an empty house. I wrestled out of my backpack and jacket, propped my feet up on the couch, and laid my head down. As the day drifted away and I began to sleep, I heard a noise coming from upstairs. It was the familiar sound of a body shifting on a bed, the floorboards complaining underneath. Then a faint, muffled sniffle.

Upstairs, my mother was curled up on her bed, her eyes red. She was still wearing her work outfit—gray blazer, pleated skirt. Her collared shirt was unbuttoned and her stockinged feet poked out from under the covers.

She had been in pain for the past two weeks. That morning, she had gone to the doctor to find out the results of her tests and had stayed in bed since. The pain had started in her chin, an aching that came out of nowhere and spread to her spine. She had had difficulty getting out of bed the past few days.

She told me how scared she was, and the tears kept coming and coming. I had to ask her to stop, to calm down, and surprisingly, she listened to me, if out of nothing else than desperation. "If they don't know what it is, why should you worry?" I asked. She smiled at me, my naïve logic seeming to calm her. She laughed softly. I kissed her, and then excused myself to go downstairs and switched on the television.

The pain continued and the doctors continued to be confounded. The air at home was decidedly anxious. Our family dinners of curries and aromatic roasts ceased. My father fixed simple, utilitarian meals that filled my stomach and suited my mother's health restrictions. I brought a tray to my mother's bedroom every evening and ate at the kitchen table with my father. He fumbled with the dishes and silverware as the sound of the TV buzzed from upstairs.

"Thank you," my mother would say as she stared at the television. She would hug me or touch my cheek, and I would look deep into her eyes, searching for something that had already gone.

At last a chain of referrals led to an oncologist. I was called to the office at school on the day of the appointment, and I was almost relieved to learn what it was, even though it was the worst possible outcome, because it ended this horrible period of not knowing.

He is waiting for me at the airport, carries my small suitcase all the way to his blue hatchback. We kiss in the car, chastely, tentatively. His apartment is on the top floor of a three-story building in King. The landlady is an old Russian woman who smokes at the bottom of the back stairwell and cries every night. She has no family and no visitors; her life is a mystery that I fill in with tragedy.

His apartment is a one-bedroom, spare, decorated with brown thrift-store furniture. It smells faintly of mothballs and cologne. In the living room are four towering bookcases. None of them match. The books overflow from the shelves, stacked in corners, piled on the coffee table. We sit in the kitchen and he makes me peppermint tea. When I finish the tea, he takes the cup from me and puts his lips to my forehead. I sigh. We embrace and sink into each other. We find our way to his small bedroom and his low platform bed. He undresses me and runs his fingertips all over my body. When we make love, it's like we are two halves of a whole joining. There is no space between us, no awkwardness. We lie in bed for many hours afterward, smiling, tracing the light from the window on each other's skin.

That evening, he takes me shopping at the neighborhood market. It is a pioneering food co-op that also runs a food bank on weekends, serving different income types in the area. We stroll down the aisles. I push the cart from behind and he steers with his hand on the front. He pauses every few steps to hold up an item. *You like this? You need this? Do you drink dairy milk? I prefer rice.* I say yes to granola, rice milk, a young organic chicken, lemon, fresh rosemary, and baby potatoes.

When he goes out for work on my third night, I take the chicken out of the fridge, wash it, and pat it dry. I load it into his only suitable baking pan. My hands shake as I grease the skin with olive oil and rub salt and pepper all over the body. My knife wriggles as I cut the lemon in half and squeeze citrus over the bird. I tear the leaves off the rosemary and dot them all over the skin, shoving the stems deep inside the cavity along with the spent lemon halves. The baby potatoes I run under the tap, trying to be gentle as I massage off the grit under warm water.

My mother taught me how to roast a chicken to succulent moistness inside and crispiness outside. She taught me that men don't always need, but they love, a woman who can cook and keep house. It wasn't sexism, she said (such a disavowal, I noted, was usually a signal that it was); domesticity was harder to find in a partner now, because of feminism, and just like a job candidate who can code HTML, it was something that set you above the others.

As I lift the chicken, covered in foil, into the oven, I worry that I have not remembered my mother's instructions correctly. Is it an hour at 350 degrees, or 400? Or do I start at 350 and then move up to 400 when I remove the foil? What if the oven is irregular? What if, no matter how perfectly I cook the chicken, he doesn't like it? Then I would be a bad feminist *and* a bad cook. I shove the bird into the oven and collapse onto the floor.

A few hours later, Peter returns home. He sets the table and pours us wine. He eats each bite through a satisfied smile, and I realize that, even if the chicken had been charred, or half-raw, I would never have known the difference from his face. To my taste, it is seasoned well but a little on the dry side.

We spend the next three days in bed except when we are carousing around the city, hand in hand, feeling like everything is brand-new and already ours.

On the plane ride home, I look at my calendar, making plans for my next visit. When I get home, I make the announcement. I call Aminah and my father. It's official, real this time: I am in love.

A morning of Internet browsing leads me down a rabbit hole of research on serial killers' wives. For every infamous man there are handfuls of women who become attached to him—who become infatuated, entangled, to small and more serious degrees. What strikes me—what is discomfiting, and what makes me return to these women long after this day—is the truly common nature of their relationships with these men. How close each of them was to death, or to the discovery of what her husband had done.

And then there are the strangest cases, of women who seek out men already accused, sometimes convicted, of crimes.

Women who have married serial killers have given several different reasons. Some believe they can change a man as cruel and powerful as a serial killer. Others "see" the little boy who the killer once was and seek to nurture him. A few hope to share in the media spotlight or get a book or movie deal.

Then there's the notion of the "perfect boyfriend." A woman knows where he is at all times and knows he's thinking about her. While she can claim that someone loves her, she does not have to endure the day-to-day issues involved in most relationships. There's no laundry to do, no cooking for him, and no accountability. She can keep the fantasy charged up for a long time.

These wives often make significant sacrifices, sometimes sitting for hours every week to await the brief face-to-face visit in prison. They might give up jobs or families to be near their soul mate, and they will certainly be spending money on him—perhaps all they have.

How common are their reasons for entering these relationships. How many times have I hungered for loyalty, for the feeling of being needed. From time to time, I wish that I could be the cause for someone to genuinely change.

I search eagerly for their photos and when I find them, I am struck by how normal and happy they look. How easily they could be someone I know. I search every inch of the pictures for hints of the horror that lurked inside their husbands, but there is nothing. There is never a hint, is there?

Death and pleasure we experience asymptotically. We spend much time working upward on the slope, and most people only sometimes approach the lines of pure pleasure or death, close enough to touch. Maybe once or twice in a lifetime, for each.

With Peter, at least some part of me is attempting to parse these experiences, to separate the liminal from the mundane, from my baseline. I need an anchor so that I'm not living so close to death anymore. I need to believe in life again.

Sex is kicking death in the ass while singing.

I don't sleep for two nights. Instead I am wide awake and tossing. Each day I feel less like the person I was the day before, my body hurtling so fast in one direction that my mind cannot keep pace. I can scarcely remember who I was before my body became like this.

I dream in bright, swirling colors. The dreams are so vivid that they linger with me long after I've woken up. I feel the same feelings that grip me at night while I'm at my desk, or on the subway. I will freeze, lost in them—scared, worried, or comforted in the same way—for hours.

I dream that I am married to my high school boyfriend, Jerome. We're living in one of the small government tract houses that are on the other, poorer side of town. Jerome is his old self: carefree, arrogant, handsome as all hell. He doesn't have a job, but goes out in the morning and doesn't come home until late at night. I question him and find out that he is sleeping with one of the popular girls from our high school, who is living in a mansion on the nicer side of town. She is married to Leonardo DiCaprio (which explains the mansion), but is as unhappy as we are. For most of the dream, I am lonely, and when I find out about the affair, I am livid. I throw a vase at Jerome's head and it breaks a hole in our living room wall. Jerome is terrified that I will kill him.

A few days later, in another dream, my mother and father are still living in my childhood home, and I am on the opposite side of town with Peter. We are happy. In this one, I am living with Peter in the same house from my dream with Jerome. My mother shows up to visit, and I am so excited to tell her about my new life. She takes me into a small bedroom at the back of the house, and I expect she will tell me how much she likes Peter and how happy she is for me. Instead, every time I try to speak to her, her image fades like she is appearing on a broken TV screen. Eventually, she fades away completely, and I'm left with nothing but the feeling of losing her all over again.

I dream that a hole opens up in the middle of the street and it swallows my father. He is just walking down the street one day, and then he is gone. I wake up crying, and there is no one for me to cry to. I spend the next few hours huddled in bed, and as soon as day breaks, I call my father.

"Ouma," he says, calling me my nickname from childhood, "everything's all right. I'm not going anywhere."

It happens again, this tightening feeling and then the nausea, when I am sitting at my desk and then again when I am vacuuming the hallway in my apartment. I realize that the paunch in my belly that normally goes away after a big meal doesn't this time. Instead it is turgid and my pelvis is sore, as if slowly being stretched apart, and I walk with my hips slightly parted, my tail angled toward the sky.

I buy a pregnancy test and it says yes.

PART TWO

Aminah and Frank had been broken up for a month when she called to tell me that she was pregnant and needed an abortion. At the time, things were okay between them, and Frank had visited her in New York. They returned to her house from a party where Frank was talking to another girl. When they came home, Aminah fucked him with all her might, desperate for his attention, and afterward she collapsed in a ball next to him, crying, drunk, in the dark. She picked a fight with him and threw him out, and he rode the bus back to D.C. in the middle of the night.

They hadn't spoken in two weeks. I caught the train up to New York that weekend. We walked to the clinic, past picketers in front, and I helped her separate her belongings at the metal detector. We were led into a cold linoleum waiting room. I took notes for her during the consultation with the nurse practitioner. As we approached the doors to the operating area, she asked the nurse's aide, "Can she come with me?" The aide refused, gently as she could, so I held Aminah's hand until I couldn't anymore. I waved to her through the swinging door.

Afterward, she told me three other women were in the recovery room with her, two black and one white. The procedures had been completed in separate operating rooms, and at the end, they all ended up in one waiting room. The women who received anesthesia were worse than the others. They were confused, getting up and falling to the ground. Aminah was awake the whole time. The procedure didn't hurt, she said, and the people were as nice and thorough as could be. But there was no getting around the discomfort. When it was over, they sat clutching their stomachs, and Aminah kept thinking about what color hair the baby would have had. Would it have looked more like Frank or like her? She didn't cry, though another woman did. The other, dazed from the drugs, inquired repeatedly about a bus schedule. None of the other women had anyone waiting for them.

Aminah said that she wasn't sad. We never raised the morality of the action, because our politics took care of that. Neither of us believed that a fetus legally constituted a human life. But Aminah still cried as if she had lost something, and I had to tell her that she was wrong, that it was nothing to begin with.

Yet part of me doubted that statement, because I was smart enough to believe that nothing on this earth could be completely knowable. That little tadpole could have feelings, and there could be a God, and we could have angered God with what we did that day.

What I knew for sure was that if I had been in Aminah's shoes, I would have chosen the same thing, and I would have mourned the same way she did. And I would have wished, against the futility of such thoughts and acceptance of my decision, that it hadn't happened, in the same way that I knew she did.

When I finally got her back into bed and fed her painkillers along with canned tomato soup, Aminah started crying, harder than I had ever seen her cry, even harder than the time she broke her ankle at camp field day in third grade and you could see the bone poking through her skin. "I love Frank," she wailed over and over, "and he's going to hate me for this."

I told her she didn't know that he would, but she decided to keep it a secret anyway. She never told him, and three months later they were back together for good.

My mother was completely exhausted in the first few weeks after treatment. She needed someone to bring her lunch during the day, to remind her to take her medicine, and to sit and watch television with her. I was home from college for the summer and played her caretaker. For most of the day, she sat alone in my parents' bed, in the same position: hugging a body pillow, her head angled toward the television. She wore a stocking cap and her old cotton pajamas.

Her treatment center was in the middle of one of Philadelphia's most expensive neighborhoods. The building was a classic stone-fronted townhouse that overlooked a small park. It looked like a mansion, offering an opulence I imagined to be comforting to my mother. But that was one thing we never talked about: the apparent moneyed-ness of her treatment. It was something she knew her friends could never afford, and for that I think she felt guilty.

She told me that, surprisingly to her, most of the people in her chemo center were black. I was surprised as well, but I never revealed as much. I thought of a friend's mom whom I knew from elementary school, and the people in the ads and brochures for cancer foundations. They had a look: older, round, rose-cheeked, what little hair they had graying, and mostly white. No, my mother said, in her center they were mostly black men and women, quite a few of them young—in their thirties and forties—working- to middle-class. Many brought their children to treatment because the kids didn't have anywhere else to go.

She told me about one black woman in her support group who had no family, no friends willing to take her in or help her. It was just her and her daughter, the woman said, and she cried and cried.

I never told my mother that, until then, I had thought of cancer as a disease of privilege. I hated how it had been elevated above and beyond all other diseases. I hated the ribbons, the bracelets, the ubiquitous awareness campaigns, the constant sponsorships.

Another thing I wouldn't tell her: Since starting college, I hadn't admitted to anyone that my mother had cancer. I didn't want anyone's pity. My classmates and I theorized enthusiastically in class about the AIDS movement, and how disease had taken the place of dictators in postcolonial Africa. I could not admit to my friends that my family was benefiting so heavily from First World wealth. They thought that in Africa we lived in huts and played with elephants. I did nothing to disabuse them of that notion. Dirty and inconvenient, AIDS was a disease of the people, I thought. Cancer, to me, was the opposite. Its cause was endorsed and healthily sponsored.

But I never admitted to my mother what I thought of her disease, that thing she lived with day and night, that was more present to her than us, than even God. Unlike family or faith, her disease was something she had never chosen. When I came close to telling her, I remembered that, and it rendered me silent.

What I felt was extremely uncomfortable, and she would have resented me for it; as much as she suffered, many other people were suffering worse. Her disease only reinforced how the world saw us: not black or white, not American or African, not poor or rich. We were confined to the middle, and would always be. As hard as she tried to separate herself from the binds of apartheid, we were still within its grip. It had become the indelible truth of our lives, and nothing—not sickness, not suffering, not death—could change that.

While she was in bed drifting in and out of sleep, I sat alone in the kitchen. The kitchen in their apartment was modern and open, with an eat-in island in the center of the room, the seats facing the oven and fridge. All of the appliances were new stainless steel, the countertops a rare pink granite. Every day I sat there, in the company only of those appliances and the sounds that they made. A bathroom was just off the kitchen, so I didn't need to leave the space at all during the day except to shower. For most of those four weeks, that was what I did.

Every morning, I set my laptop on the island and did not leave except to bring my mother her meals. I rarely worked or wrote e-mails. I avoided anything that would connect me with the outside world, which felt too out of control. Instead, I retreated into the apartment and watched the world go by like a parade. The kitchen was my world. I ate gluttonously and gained ten pounds.

I passively read my e-mails. Most were from college, asking me to choose my classes, to sign up for health insurance. I let the deadlines pass and later received red-lettered alerts from deans and other administrators. I began to enjoy taking those multiple-choice surveys on the Internet. *What movie star's hair do you have? What movie is your love life?*

My mother refused to go outside except for doctors'

appointments. Her pills didn't seem to help the pain. The only things I could give her were her meals.

The refrigerator was the center of my kitchen world. It sat right across from me, about as tall as a regular human, and when the radio was off, its hum was the only sound in the room.

When I first arrived back home, I cleaned it out furiously, tossing all the old takeout boxes and the stagnant leftovers of curries and meats. I threw away anything with a large amount of oil or fat and duplicates of condiments—extra bottles of ketchup, mustard, mayonnaise. I scrubbed every shelf and surface until the inside gleamed.

I restocked the fridge with healthy foods: fruits, vegetables, yogurts, soy milk, probiotic this and that. When it was done, and the fridge was filled with vibrant colors and smelled of Lysol, I felt lifted, hopeful. I understood then, awash in unfiltered refrigerator light, that this was how I was going to cure my mom, with whole grains and elbow grease.

But one by one, the old food reinvaded the fridge. Every visitor who came by (and there were many) brought us a different dish. Curries, stews, fried rice. The things that were meant to stick to the bones, to comfort. The foods my mother loved best. Friends gave them to us in their own pots with no mention of when the pots should be returned.

During my second week back home, my mom's best friend stopped by. She brought us a pork roast, mashed potatoes, and beans, all wrapped in tinfoil. She gave them to me to pack in the fridge. I had to take my vegetables out of the crisper and set them in the fruit bowl in the middle of the island, defenseless.

I took the huge tinfoil packages, the grease beginning to leak through, and shoved them in the spotless drawer. I slammed the door shut and ran straight to the spare bedroom. I locked myself inside, buried my face in the bed pillows, and cried.

A week before I was supposed to begin college again, I called the dean's office and told the administration I wouldn't be coming for next semester.

"You'll be returning after that," my father commanded.

"Yes," I said, but the truth was that I didn't know anything for sure anymore.

A story came up on the local news about a murder not far from our house in a much rougher neighborhood where this type of thing was ordinary, almost expected. The news was filled with stories from those blocks, faces of its children alternately lost, made criminal, locked away. They showed a man's picture—he was dark-skinned, with a white beard and white eyebrows, a friendly smile. He looked around my mother's age. He was a mail carrier for a neighborhood in the south. He went out in the morning to work, and on his way to the subway, he was jumped by two thieves. He refused to give up his wallet and cell phone and they shot him. He died on the sidewalk.

My mother turned to me with surprising calm. She spoke as if she were discussing someone else's life, someone else's mother.

"He's just like me," she mused. "I'll die too, it's just that how I'll go is more decided."

"Yes, Mom," I said, and we turned back to the news. More deaths, more robberies, life went on.

My mother was unable to stay in the bedroom any longer. She could barely sit up on her own, and it was too difficult for us to move her on their old king-sized bed. A social worker came to the apartment and walked through each of the rooms, occasionally stopping to take a measurement and scratch the figure down on her clipboard. Two days later, a large truck pulled up outside our building and, an hour later, a hospital bed was set up in our living room.

The hospital bed was stiff, menacing. It looked institutional and cold amid the warm colors of our living room walls, hung with my mother's African tapestries, blankets, and textiles that were her pride and joy. When we first brought her into the living room, my mother resisted.

"It pains my back," she said in her confused, drug-addled English. She insisted on sleeping on the couch. My father or I slept in the hospital bed instead.

She woke up several times during the night needing medicine or help going to the toilet. I would switch on the light, pull the plastic commode next to her, lift her off the couch, and then pull her back onto the couch. The whole process took around fifteen minutes, and once it was completed, we were up for the next hour. I barely slept during the nights I tended to her, so I rested alternate nights while my father took the replacement shift.

One night while on my shift, I was awoken by my mother's bald head hovering over me. Half asleep, I was happy to see her standing for the first time in months.

"I want to go home," she said.

She paced around the bed, possessed by some strange, dark energy.

"You are home." I got to my feet and walked after her. She began crying and tearing at her clothes.

She ripped at the few stray hairs that dotted her scalp. She walked faster, and I had to chase her to the other side of the living room. When I finally caught my mother, I hugged her to me. She was shaking, sweaty. I rubbed her back, trying to calm her.

"I miss my father," she said.

I realized to which home she was referring. I realized she would never see South Africa again, her father, brothers and sisters, her many friends. At times during the day I felt heroic, but then I felt small, worthless. I would never do this for her.

Eventually I coaxed her into the bed and curled up beside her. The bed was so narrow that we never would have fit on it together when she was healthy. I tried to find words that would fill the space that her home had left, but there was nothing.

"I'm tired, Mom," I whispered as I dozed off.

My father and I didn't communicate much except to coordinate nurse visits for my mother or to give updates on her medicines. We were holding so much in, our pain distinct from each other's in many ways. I suppose we thought that if we ever acknowledged this, all our carefully assembled control would fall to pieces. I was terrified of his pain—that of losing a lifelong partner, so many years tossed out the window. And I'm sure he feared the destabilization of my loss—how much of my life yet to live would be marred by this trauma.

Because my father was a man and relatively young, a part of me was scared that he would leave. That was always the fear with men. I suppose this was a part of the not talking, the not crying. I thought that if I didn't acknowledge the horror we were living in, it somehow wouldn't be as bad, and he would stay.

But day after day he didn't leave, and his eyes never wavered from my mother when she was wheeled out of the hospital, or lifted into the car, or when she was being sutured or changed or intubated. So many times when I couldn't look anymore, he did.

In my nights off shift from caring for my mother, I started to troll online dating sites and personal ads. I found Liz and Patrick's ad in the personals section on Craigslist. They were a young couple in West Philly, on the opposite side of town from my parents' apartment. They were looking for a third "for occasional fun and spice." From our e-mails and phone conversations, they seemed intelligent and polite. They told me they both worked at the state office and were only two years older than me. I told them I was a teacher at a school near the university where I'd once tutored.

When I arrived at their apartment, they welcomed me in and we shared a glass of wine in their small kitchen. The house—a wood-shingled Victorian divided into three units—had the same layout as Dean's. The kitchen sat just off the bedroom, the dining alcove in the same spot. I pictured him and the thin girl at the kitchen sipping wine, his limbs slowly interlacing with hers. I took a big sip from my glass, closed my eyes, stanched the thought.

Patrick asked about my school, my work. I stitched together an answer based on the one session of half-assed tutoring I did in my first year of college. I told him I was a math teacher, and I was relieved when he stopped there. Any more and I would have been exposed. To my surprise, they remained smiling in front of me, then reassuringly at each other until Liz summoned Patrick into the living room, where I heard them whispering. They returned to the kitchen.

"Why don't we move to the bedroom?" Patrick said.

In the bedroom, there was a camera set up to the side of the bed. I saw the red light blinking, already turned on.

"Is this all right?" Liz asked.

I wasn't sure if it was. She kissed me and we fell to the bed. Patrick joined in, tearing our clothes off like we were Christmas presents. We made love for two hours, and when it was done I was satisfied, but more important, my mind was empty, my lips tingling.

I fell asleep and awoke at dawn. I dressed while Liz and Patrick were still sleeping, their arms crossed over each other. I caught the 7:00 a.m. bus back over to my side of town. My father would be eating breakfast then, almost ready to leave for work. From the bus, I watched the sun rise over city hall. The bus was nearly empty. There was no one around to see me cry.

That night, I didn't eat. I collapsed early and slept into the late morning. My father spent the night at the hospital with my mother while I rested at home. My father called from the hospital in the morning to say that my mother had had an accident.

He was in the hospital room, waiting with the nurses to decide their next move. He lowered his voice so that no one else could hear.

"Can you bring me a change of clothes?" he said.

She had peed all over the bed and her clothes, and when he tried to clean the mess before the nurses came in, it got all over him. His voice cracked, and he began to cry. He put the phone down.

I packed him a shirt and sweater from his closet and some new pants from his drawer. I headed to the hospital, fighting off the image of my mother and father covered in her piss.

By the time I arrived, they had fitted her with a catheter tube.

"No more accidents," the male nurse said, smiling, trying to be upbeat. I imagined the painful method by which he had connected the catheter to my mother's bladder. From the bottom of her blanket ran a tube connected to a clear plastic container tied to the foot of her bed.

I sat in a chair by her right side while my dad changed in the bathroom in the hall. When he returned, the doctors told us she wouldn't wake up after this. I wondered if she could hear, if she knew what was going on, and I decided it was better if she didn't. I decided not to think anymore. I stared at the urinal, the tubing, not watching, not reacting. The room smelled acrid because she had a bacterial infection, which was forcing her into a coma. I let the smell overwhelm me until I couldn't smell it anymore. The stench was nothing more than molecules moving in and out of my nostrils, the scene nothing more than light reflected off objects alive and inanimate, some dying.

We moved her to a hospice in downtown Philadelphia, across the street from one of the cafés I used to visit when I was a teenager. She was taken there from the hospital by ambulance, by two young women around my age—one of them larger, darker-skinned, with hair gelled to her forehead in plastic-looking curlicues. They wore smiles to which I had no concept of how to respond and joked in a careful way with me and my dad. I imagined them being trained to handle families with extreme sensitivity: *You can use humor, but not too much. Stick to neutral subjects, nothing controversial.*

My father rode in the ambulance while I waited outside the hospital, under the neon EMERGENCY sign. After I'd spent twenty minutes in the cold, my mother's best friend pulled up in front of me in her old Chrysler.

She cried as she turned the wheel, almost running red lights. We didn't speak. Her car smelled stale, of smoke. The oldies station played on the radio: Al Green beneath a light layer of static.

The hospice was a new place on the top floor of a cold brick building with few windows. When we arrived, a tie-dyed social worker tried to steer me into a cheerily lit kids' room. The staff had a phrase for what was happening to my mom—"the dying process"—and they said the words like they should be followed by a ™. Like she was in the process of walking to the store or buying groceries. Just another thing that humans do.

While my father was out grabbing us prepared sandwiches for dinner, I crept into her room. I closed the door and shoved a chair against the doorknob so no one could enter. I had many things I wanted to say. Some sleepless nights ago, I'd made a list of all the things I needed to apologize for, all the things I needed to tell her I forgave her for. But as I stood there with those mathematics in hand, the weight of the moment on me, I said nothing. And when I tried to speak, only tears came. The pain was exponential. Because as much as I cried, she could not comfort me, and this fact only multiplied my pain. I realized that this would be life; to figure out how to live without her hand on my back; her soft, accented English telling me *Everything will be all right, Thandi.* This was the paradox: How would I ever heal from losing the person who healed me? The question was so enormous that I could see only my entire life, everything I know, filling it.

They gave me a stapled book on "the dying process." I read about symptoms that occur in people who are dying. It described what to expect at intervals of months, weeks, and days before a person dies from illness or old age. It said that the person will stop eating meat, and then vegetables, and then they will be able to eat only a few bites of very soft food. And then they will eat nothing. They will sleep most of the day, with their eyes half open and unseeing, glassy. As the person begins to sleep more hours of the day than they are awake, they will become disoriented, as their dreams become merged with our world, and they prepare to live in the other world—the afterlife—forever.

The book told me that people behave in death as they do in life. The more relaxed we are in life, the more free of stress, the more likely we are to go quickly. The fearful, and those with unfinished business, will cling to life as long as possible, afraid to enter the next stage. Protective parents, it says, belong to this group. They will struggle to the very end, unwilling or unable to leave their children behind.

From the list of symptoms, I realized that my mother had been dying for months. Sometimes I would stand in the doorway of her room watching her, waiting for her chest to rise to make sure she wasn't dead. I was afraid to watch, but also afraid to leave. I realized that as much as I was holding on, she was too.

My mother died between Thanksgiving and Christmas, the final cruel stroke of this whole experience. I will hate the holidays for the rest of my life.

At home, in my family's empty apartment, my father and I pulled the two-foot-tall Christmas tree from the back of our supply closet, and shoved it into a corner, and plugged it in with begrudging acknowledgment.

Aminah invited me to her family's house for their annual tree trimming party. They all hugged me and said the right things, and at the end of the night, Aminah and I found ourselves alone in the basement. We sat in front of the fire, a couple glasses of wassail in. I cried openly in front of her, so much that my snot dribbled down my lip. She laughed.

"Can I stay here forever?" I asked her, feeling, for the first time, warm and comforted.

"Of course," she answered. But I didn't. I didn't even stay the night. I had another glass of wine and carefully drove home through the dark, snow-covered streets.

We received a pamphlet in the mail called "What We Lose: A Support Guide," published by the hospice. It had tips on what foods to eat, the constant exhortations to exercise, the expected warnings against caffeine and alcohol. And one page had this glossary of terms:

Grief is a response to loss. It is a process, describing how one feels and thinks.

Mourning describes how a person expresses their loss.

Bereavement is the event of loss. It is also a change in status; when a husband loses his wife and becomes a widower, or a child loses a parent and becomes an orphan.

I lingered on that word, "orphan." An orphan was always a person without parents, without roots. I had one parent, and one was not none.

Orphan (noun)

1: a young animal that has lost its mother

2: one deprived of some protection or advantage, such as "*orphans* of the storm"

3: a child deprived by death of one or usually both parents

But the condition isn't mathematical. The loss is what creates the condition. It's not the fact of one parent, but that the loss has occurred.

It's the wound, not the parts that are left untouched.

She left us with no debts. Three closets full of clothes and shoes, sixty-three pieces of jewelry—precious, semiprecious, and costume. And other things.

My mother loved buying kitchen tools of any type, from measuring cups to appliances, small and large. Aprons, place mats, napkins. Cutlery with handles shaped as objects—branches, small animals, even human hands. She marveled at the variety, as she did with most things available in America. In South Africa, everything was utilitarian. They didn't have so many gadgets, so many different types of one thing. Choice. This was the biggest advantage America offered, even though she recognized that it was not always good. (This was also the problem with my generation, of course.)

A cache of prescription narcotics had to be disposed of at the hospital, carefully logged by the pharmacists, and signed by us.

When I was a child, my mother would try to convince me of a woman's need for a secret stash. "It can be anything: land, property, even a couple hundred dollars. You know, in case anything goes wrong and you have to get the hell out of there." Her mother had told her this, as her mother before had told her. When I insisted that things were different in America, that we have laws to protect assets in divorce and alimony and women's refuges, she just smiled at me knowingly. I knew to expect a surprise, but I didn't know how big the surprise would be.

Aside from her retirement fund, savings, and investments, my mom kept small amounts of cash socked away in separate accounts, some in tiny sums, others in fairly unbelievable numbers. We divided the money, per her will, evenly between me and my father. Even though I was the daughter and he was her husband, she didn't want to show favoritism. When we finally accounted for all the money and divvied it up, my father and I sat facing the sum in the lawyer's office, almost unbelieving.

Most of the clothes we gave away, to either her best friend or Goodwill. We shipped certain pieces of her jewelry to South Africa, sealing each one in a plastic bag and marking it with the name of the cousin or aunt to whom it was assigned. They sent us enthusiastic letters thanking us for the gifts, no matter their value. My aunt even called us crying. It was such an easy thing—a relief, even—to get rid of the stuff, but the gesture meant everything to them. And that feeling extended to us also. We were all they had left of her.

I put my share of the money in an investment account that could be accessed only by a phone call. I swore to myself that I would lock the money away, like she did when she saved it, and keep it safe. This was all I had left of her.

I read in "What We Lose" that the bereaved need human touch. Aminah booked me a massage at a yoga studio in Philadelphia. I had a sixty-minute session with the lead therapist, who came into my appointment from her afternoon vinyasa class, still sweating. She oiled me up and rubbed me down expertly, pulling my joints back into place, mincing my back, all the while explaining the purpose of each of her movements. She untwisted my body and my mind, which she explained was like a giant overworked muscle, in control of every other muscle in my body, respondent to all its stresses and limitations.

With each stroke and crack, tears came, until they flooded out the center of the headrest. When she stood over me, my tears dripped onto her bare foot, and she lifted my head. I told her that it wasn't long ago, what happened. She hugged me. Reedy instrumental music played in the background. My towel fell away from my chest. She rocked me back and forth like my mother used to. Her body was hard and toned, and I cried because I would never feel my mother's big soft breast again.

Unexpected events—UFOs, ghosts—can be explained by subjective experience. A person has lost a pet and is distracted with loneliness day after day. She is so sad over the cat's death that she doesn't leave the house and can only stay indoors, thinking about the way the cat used to dart across the floor, from couch to table to armchair, and under the windowsill.

One day, she is sitting and watching the window in her living room, thinking of the cat. The curtain covers a window that is thin and leaky, and outside the sky is gray, brewing a thunderstorm. She can hear the wind whistling, and it makes her think of the days she would sit inside, shielded from the cold, with the cat curled peacefully on her lap. She sees the curtain flutter, and thinks of the way the cat would walk on the windowsill and flutter the curtains in the same exact way. This could easily be explained by the wind, but because her mind is overwhelmed with grief for her lost companion, she imagines, convinced, that it is the spirit of the cat.

A ghost is not a fact in itself; rather, it is a symbol for a need. The most important aspect of the ghost is the need that creates it. The cat-ghost is a symbol of the woman's grief.

A series of small miracles started to happen around us. A South African friend who worked at my mom's hospital received a long-prayed-for promotion that he often went to my mother for advice about. Two weeks after my mother's funeral, after a months-long wait, a cousin who had suffered as an undocumented immigrant for twelve years finally received approval for her green card. Both people credited these events as gifts sent to them by my mother from heaven.

Aminah and Frank took a long-planned vacation to Vietnam a month to the day after my mother's funeral. Two days before they left, I cleared out the downstairs storage closet. Aminah called on her way to Best Buy to purchase a new DSLR camera for the trip.

"Frank wants to take pictures of the temples, with all the intricate carvings," she told me.

I was going through my mother's old things. It was a mix of old jackets, work papers, and her beloved kitchen tools. Not five minutes after I hung up the phone, I came across an old Sharper Image box, unopened. She often fell for the siren song of the pictures in the retailer's catalog and the ease of automated ordering by phone. She would order gadget after gadget and stow them in the downstairs closet still in their boxes, forgetting that she'd bought them. Inside the box was a brand-new DSLR camera, still in the plastic. I called up Aminah and she came over right away to borrow it.

On their trip, Frank proposed to Aminah in front of a temple, and after she accepted, they posed for a picture, with her ring finger to the camera to show off the diamond. A local boy pressed the shutter button of my mom's camera.

There is the logical conclusion: My family and friends experienced a string of positive coincidences at this particular time in our lives. Then there is the supernatural one, which we chose to believe—my mother, or the power of the universe in recognition of her death, influenced a positive outcome in each of these events to better us.

I made the choice to believe in my mother's spirit. I chose to create a ghost, for the purpose of my own comfort. It made me happy to think that my mother still existed somewhere and that she could help us right after her passing.

Skepticism says that ghosts are merely unexplained phenomena. In our culture, "unexplained" = "explained as a ghost."

Whether or not ghosts exist is beside the point. The methods relied upon for their proof are all shoddy, and even in the most certain of circumstances explanations are too easily disproved, subverted by one's subjectivity. The woman created the cat-ghost out of the moving curtains.

My theory is that loneliness creates the feeling of haunting.

I did my best to wake up while my father was leaving the house. I thought that if I could be up by six thirty, and see him even for a few minutes, I would feel less lonely, terrified as I was by the emptiness of their airy apartment. The antique furniture, the African artifacts and trinkets carefully chosen by my mother's hand . . . they all seemed to breathe and sigh her name. I hoped seeing his face would make the house not feel so large, the empty space not so enervating.

But I tossed at night, every night, until the early morning, and with nowhere to be the next day, I was never awake before noon.

As soon as I got out of the shower, I packed a book in my bag and headed to my coffee shop for breakfast. I dawdled and stalled, ordering coffee upon coffee so that I wouldn't have to go home. I read the question on the baristas' faces: *Doesn't she have somewhere else to be?* When the coffee shop closed, I would finally leave and spend the rest of the day cruising around the city in my car until it was time for my father to come home from work. Then I returned home, exhausted and lonely.

The things seemed to happen only during the day, when the apartment was empty except for me. The thermostat found itself all the way up at 73, the temperature my mother liked, too hot for me or my father. The vents puttered from the heating pipes, and it sounded just like my mother's breath.

I hated to be alone in that apartment so much that I started showering at night, to shorten my time in the mornings. I zipped straight from my bed, washed my face, put on a change of clothes, and headed straight out the door. I made sure to come home after eight, nine on days when my father had staff meetings.

Soon my father started inquiring into my plans. *When will you return to school? Perhaps you should find something to occupy your time during the day.* He asked the questions halfheartedly, with little interest in my answers, and I began to realize that he was doing this out of duty—some workaholic's ideal of busyness—and not because he was actually concerned. Most days, his eyes were empty, and I continued to avoid his gaze because I was afraid of what lurked behind.

We stopped eating dinner together every evening. Most nights, our fridge was empty. We stopped sending out our annual holiday cards with a family photo, or thoughtful, hand-lettered *Thank You* notes when we received a gift. Holidays were a wash. The two-foot plastic tree became the norm—my father didn't purchase a single new tree after my mother died. All the plants in the house withered away shortly after the funeral, their brethren never to enter our household.

Before, the guiding instinct of our family was strongly intuitive, compassionate, and nurturing. In a word, maternal. My father and I both became orphans, malnourished, emotionally distant, neglected. Often, when we were sitting in the kitchen eating our takeout dinners, each of us at our separate spots—me on my laptop at the island, my father paging through a magazine at the table—we seemed barely recognizable to me. I looked at us and thought, whose family is this?

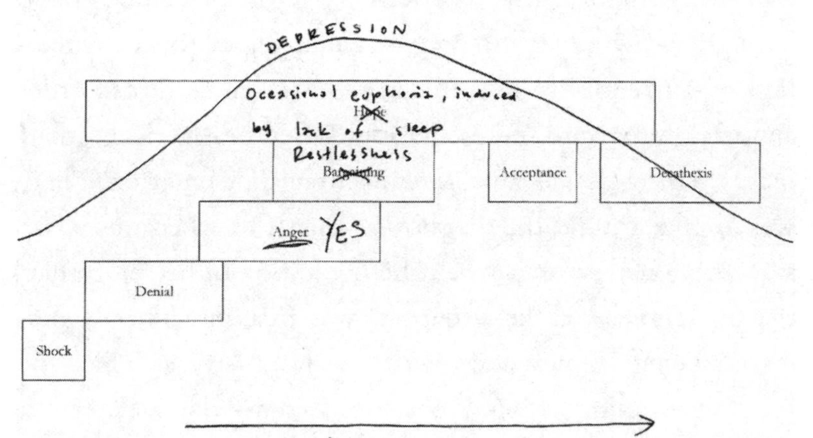
DEPRESSION
Occasional euphoria, induced by lack of sleep
Hope
Restlessness
Bargaining
Acceptance
Decathexis
Anger
YES
Denial
Shock
time

When I visualized my emotions, I would picture a graph. Sometimes I would try to draw it, and it helped to see my feelings organized into a neat line, a process that connoted order and straightforward representation. When I drew the graph, I pictured the x-axis as time, the y as strength of emotion. There was a spike around the diagnosis, when I first became aware something was wrong, when the suggestion of her mortality, the uncertainty of the situation, was first introduced, and, by virtue of its newness, was especially severe. Then the line went down, when I became used to the idea, and I was too wrapped up in the details—treatments, prognoses, outcomes—to be in touch with the emotion. My return home was another spike, and after that, a steady, slow climb, at high altitude, until her death.

At the point of her death, the line circles inward into itself to infinity, disappearing into infinite fractions. It was so beyond comprehension and feeling that it wasn't able to be captured on a plane of "hurt" or "sadness," or any single human emotion.

Loss is a straightforward equation: 2 − 1 = 1. A person is there, then she is not. But a loss is beyond numbers, as well as sadness, and depression, and guilt, and ecstasy, and hope, and nostalgia—all those emotions that experts tell us come along with death. Minus one person equals all of these, in unpredictable combinations. It is a sunny day that feels completely gray, and laughter in the midst of sadness. It is utter confusion. It makes no sense.

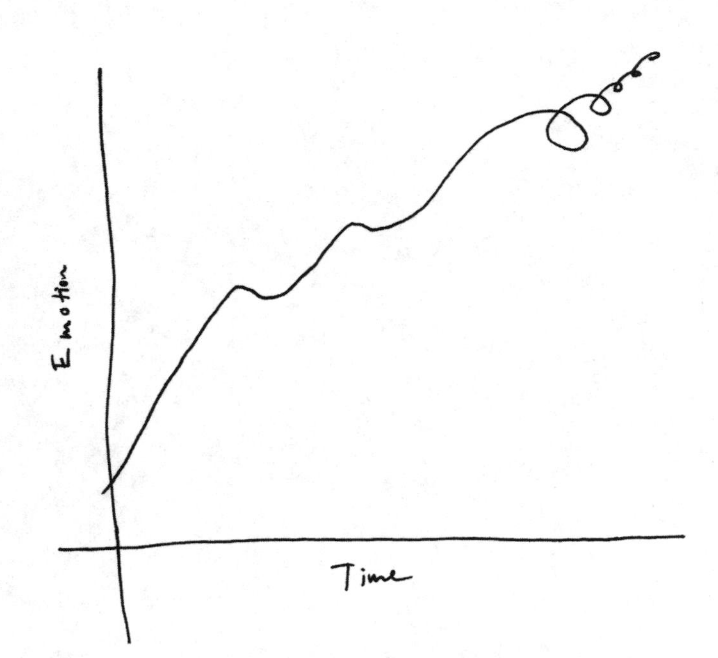
Emotion
Time

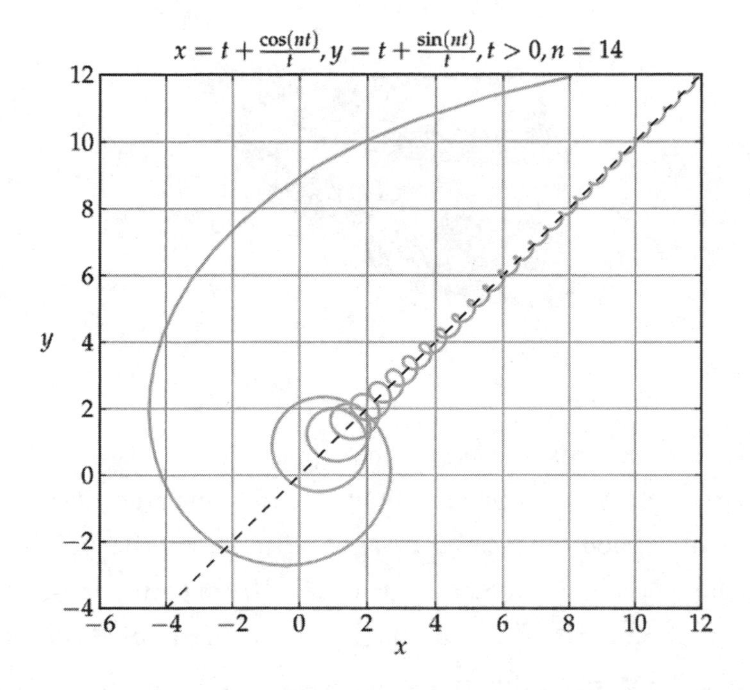

My graph resembled the form of an asymptote, the mathematical equivalent of ineffability: an object attempting to approach a line but forever failing. In the same way, my mind was trying to reconcile my new reality and failing, over and over again.

Asymptote: This appears to be a paradox to beginners in geometry, who are generally unable to imagine it possible that two lines should continue to approach one another forever, without absolute contact. But this arises from their confounding the thing called a straight line in practice (which is not a straight line, but a thin stroke of black lead or ink, as the case may be) with the straight line of geometry, which has neither breadth nor thickness, but only length. And they also imagine that if two lines might be asymptotic, the fact might be made visible, which is impossible, unless the eye could be made to distinguish any distance, however small. But if the unassisted eye cannot detect a white space between two black lines, unless that space is a thousandth of an inch in breadth, which is about the truth, it is evident that two geometrical surfaces with asymptotic boundaries, such as ABC, DEC, would appear to coincide from the point where the distance between them is about the thousandth part of an inch. The idea of a geometrical asymptote is therefore an effort of pure reason, and the possibility of it must be made manifest to the mind, not to the senses.

We will see that the same cannot be said for the sublime feeling. The relation of thinking to the object presented breaks down. In sublime feeling, nature no longer "speaks" to thought through the "coded writing" of its forms. Above and beyond the formal qualities that induced the quality of taste, thinking grasped by the sublime feeling is faced, "in" nature, with quantities capable only of suggesting a magnitude or a force that exceeds its power of presentation. This powerlessness makes thinking deaf or blind to natural beauty. Divorced, thinking enters a period of celibacy. It can still employ nature, but to its own end. It becomes the user of nature. This "employment" is an abuse, a violence. It might be said that in the sublime feeling, thinking becomes impatient, despairing, disinterested in attaining the ends of freedom by means of nature.

If there is a person who has never eaten a tangerine or a durian fruit, however many images or metaphors you give him, you cannot describe to him the reality of those fruits. You can do only one thing: give him a direct experience. You cannot say: "Well, the durian is a little bit like the jackfruit or like a papaya." You cannot say anything that will describe the experience of a durian fruit. The durian fruit goes beyond all ideas and notions. The same is true of a tangerine. If you have never eaten a tangerine, however much the other person loves you and wants to help you understand what a tangerine tastes like, they will never succeed by describing it. The reality of the tangerine goes beyond ideas. Nirvana is the same; it is the reality that goes beyond ideas. It is because we have ideas about nirvana that we suffer. Direct experience is the only way.

I am most troubled when my mother is very present to me, when I dream of her extra vividly and can hear her voice. Even when I wake up I am left with the eerie sensation of how I used to feel—scared, loving, and small, in comparison—in her presence.

In these moments, I feel that she is still alive and I am talking to her in my mind. But now she cannot answer back. I feel that I have some kind of beautiful secret. I love this new magical Mom who is always watching over me, whose counsel I can seek in an instant, whose advice frequently matches my own wishes and desires.

I don't know how to place this new mother, my dead mother, with the mother who was alive. When I look at her grave, I feel it the most. How can she be there when she is still here, inside me?

My mother is dead. But I still see her. But I still feel her. I can still hear her voice, even right now as I am speaking to you.

But she is dead.

When I look at this picture of her at the beach, I can feel the sun on my skin. I can hear the way she spoke to me.

But she is gone.

I can dream her, and I can hear her cry. She tells me what happened that day, and she cries with me. She tells me not to be afraid.

But she is dead.

A part of her is still alive in me.

But she is gone.

She will live forever in heaven.

But she is not on earth.

Parts of her will live on in the trees and the streams and the birds of tomorrow. She is the water and the plants and the bits of dust I see swirl in columns of light.

But she is dead.

If I look long enough at a flower, I can see the color of her cheeks in the stigma.

But she is not here.

Peter comes to New York to decide what we are going to do. This magnitude of decision cannot be made over the phone; that is the one thing we agree on.

I leave work early to pick him up from the airport. When we get back to my place, I make us steaks. Halfway into cooking them, I realize that iron is one of those tastes pregnancy will make me abhor. He eats his steak and mine and we barely speak. I just sit there and watch him chew. I eat cereal.

We sit on the small floral couch in my living room, his hands wrapped around my waist. He lowers his head to my lap, his nose nuzzling my belly. I tell him that I'm afraid I won't be a good mother, but I'm also afraid that I'll let the time pass by, and I'll never become a mother at all. We look up phone numbers and procedures on the Internet, and I tell him about the time with Aminah in college. I cry myself asleep in his arms.

On Saturday, we go through all our finances. Peter's job is junior level. His pay is barely comfortable for a single person. He says he can leave the position, find a job in finance or at a bank. I see how sad this makes him look and tell him that he doesn't need to. He tells me he has $1,000 in the bank, but he has just finished paying off his loans. The last part he says with such uncamouflaged pride, I can only sigh. My job keeps me afloat, but, living in New York City, I have no money left for savings. This brings us to another topic: Where will we live? I realize that one of the things I love so much about him might end up being the thing that keeps us apart: He loves Portland. And I love the East Coast. Neither of us will easily give up our respective homes.

The Sunday is beautiful, sunny and warm, and I wake late in the day to find Peter still sleeping next to me. In the noon light, I think I finally see him fully. He isn't a spectacular man. He isn't someone my father or even Aminah would be impressed with. My mother would lament his lack of upper-body strength and bank account. "Despite what you preach, Thandi," she would say, "you have expensive tastes." He is an ordinary man. He slowly stirs awake, smiling impossibly at me, as if we have been transported back in time, weeks before this situation occurred.

We don't speak of the pregnancy today, but instead spend the daylight hours strolling around New York's parks arm in arm. Peter has never been to the city before. He is surprised by the amount of green space we have and insists we hit up at least three parks. He marvels at every bit of nature as if it's a rare find. "You have squirrels here?" he exclaims as we see one dart by. By the end of the day, he is annoyed with them.

It is an immaculate fall day, uncharacteristically warm, tempting many to come out in T-shirts. Some women wear bikinis and sunbathe on towels. We snarl to each other looking at these exhibitionists.

In my favorite park in Brooklyn, we find a spot on the hill

from which we can see the rest of the borough sloping away from us.

It's one of my favorite places, in part because nearly everyone here looks like me. There are mixed families all around us; all of their children look like they could be mine. Peter, I feel, notices this too, and I think it makes him uncomfortable. I try to talk to him about the baby again, but he tells me he is thirsty. He goes to the store to buy us bottled water. Next to me, a family with an Asian mother and black father play. There is an infant in a stroller and a girl of maybe five with wild curls and caramel skin who looks like my young cousin. As Peter returns to my side, I smile at her, and she approaches us, carrying a sycamore leaf that is as big as her head. Her parents look on consentingly, full of Brooklyn laissez-faire. She lays the paperlike leaf in my lap.

"Wow, it's beautiful," I tell her with the animation one reserves for small children. "Thank you."

Peter takes the leaf from me, turns the stem between his fingers, and lets it fall to the ground.

"I don't think I can do this," he says. "It's just not the right time. For me or for us."

A light has been growing inside me since the park, a light that felt sure this would work out.

"Yeah, of course," I say. "That's what I was thinking."

"I'm sorry I can't be here with you. I have to get back to work." He writes me a check for $700.

I take him to the airport that evening. I get out of the driver's seat and we hug and kiss in the loading lane. Then we say goodbye.

We returned to Johannesburg one year after my mother died. Of the two weeks we spent there, I spent one afternoon with my grandfather. He sat in his recliner, in front of the TV, switched to the cricket game, and I halfheartedly arranged papers, went to the store to buy milk, and brought him cups of tea.

"You don't seem well," he said.

I laughed and said that I was fine.

"My feet ache," he said, pointing down at his blue velvet slippers. His diabetes caused his feet to swell, and they caused him great pain. I removed the slippers and found his skin dry and red. His toenails were black.

"Papa . . ."

"I'm in pain every day," he said. "It's not just my feet, it's all over."

I saw his eyes fill with tears and then looked away quickly. My father had spent most of his time in Johannesburg with my grandfather, running him all over town, sitting with him, talking. They had always gotten along, but now they behaved as old friends, reunited after a long time apart. They shared a bond over my mother's death that the rest of us couldn't know. My grandfather's pain was as unknowable to me as my father's but multiplied several times over. I was afraid that if I looked into his eyes, I might see what it was like to lose a child. Instead, I excused myself to the bathroom.

"I'll get you some muscle rub, Da."

In the small room lined by eggshell tiles, unchanged since my mother bathed in there as a baby, I gazed at his neat arrangement of ointments and creams, the same bottles that he'd used since I was a child. I cried until I felt so empty that I knew no more would come, and then I went back outside.

We assembled at my family's gravesite, at the large coloured cemetery a few minutes from my grandparents' house. As we walked from our cars to the small plot marked by a few lines of white folding chairs, I remembered my grandmother's funeral, held here ten years ago. My grief had been simple and remote. I had had no clue of the depth of feeling beneath my own mother's tears; this time I finally did.

My mother's brother Bertie led the ceremony. He had made a small fortune and a name for himself by opening a string of gas stations in coloured townships that employed neighborhood people and quietly exploited them. He walked to the front of the group with a serious look that bordered on a smirk. He could barely contain his glee at being in front of a captive audience. He rubbed his belly with a gold ring–laden hand; his children sniffed loudly from the front row.

Bertie took the urn holding my mother's ashes from the

pedestal nearby. He handed it to my grandfather, who laid it in a small hole next to my grandmother's headstone.

My cousin Lyndall squeezed my hand.

"I hope his fat ass falls in that hole," she whispered under her breath to me. We both laughed, and Bertie's children—clad in designer clothes and shades, comforted by their respective spouses—shot us disapproving stares. Though we were close as children, our relationship became distant when my cousins became certifiably rich, in a way none of us could really understand; it ended completely when they married. Their wealth made them paranoid. They closed ranks against people or conflicts that challenged any one of them. The rest of us saw this happen, felt a different kind of grief for the people they had once been.

I started to sob in huge bursts again, felt my face getting hot.

"Are you okay?" Lyndall whispered to me.

I felt Stephanie, my older cousin, poke me in the back. She opened her palm and revealed a small blue pill.

"For your nerves," Lyndall said.

I held it in my hand.

"Don't think about it," Lyndall said, and raised my hand to my mouth.

The pill kicked in just as Bertie waddled back to his seat, and everything turned gray. I stopped crying. We waited in line to throw dirt on my mother's ashes. I held my father's hand. We said our final prayer and went back the way we had come.

My cousin Lyndall is beautiful and wild. She has wavy sandy-brown hair flowing down to her back that she flicks off of her neck mischievously whenever she is lying. She's the pariah of our family because in high school, her parents caught her doing tik. They screamed and beat her and she didn't apologize, so they sent her to rehab in Botswana for a month. She came back wilder than ever, but better at hiding it.

Lyndall is that fatal mix of beautiful and visible brokenness that made all the guys swarm us whenever we would go out. When I first arrived, she took me out into the small rectangle of my grandfather's backyard and handed me a joint. As we hunched under the clothesline, Lyndall held the garments away from our smoke. "Aish, if my mother smells this I'm in for it." I chided Lyndall, still a captive to her parents' old ways. For the millionth time, I told her she should move to America. No one as free as her should live in this country. She waved off the weed smoke.

"This is dangerous," Lyndall said, putting the joint between her teeth. She led me up to the roof of our grandfather's garage just like she did when we were kids. We hoisted ourselves onto the wall, then onto the storm pipe, and up onto the tin roof.

"Papa used to hate us doing this, hey?" Lyndall said with the joint still in her teeth, casting a cautious glance into the living room window. When we were little, our grandfather had a sixth sense for our mischief. As soon as we put a foot on the house's whitewashed wall, he would be at the window, yelling threats at us to get down.

A dog barked. We lay side by side, blowing smoke into the air. We could hear pots clanging in the kitchen sink, our aunties cleaning up the funeral lunch.

"Do you remember when we were little," Lyndall said, "when we used to pretend we were grown-up? You always wanted to be twenty years old and living in New York."

"I did," I said, chuckling. "We used to practice putting on lipstick and kissing our pillows."

"I was going to marry a footballer," Lyndall purred, drawing long on the joint. "I still can."

We laughed.

"How you doing, really?" Lyndall asked.

"How do you think?" I sighed. "It feels like everything has fallen apart."

"Your mom and I were close in a—different kind of way."

My mother generally disapproved of Lyndall's wild behavior, but there was some part of her that obviously identified with it. They called each other often to share gossip, and when Lyndall got in trouble, my mother would be the first to call and chastise her. But at the end of the conversation, they would end up laughing.

I looked over and Lyndall was crying. She wiped her eyes on her forearm, the joint in her fingers.

"*Ahhhh!*" She flicked the joint off the roof. "It's time to get out of here and get drunk!"

From an article on a planned high-rise in Maboneng, the fast-developing neighborhood in Johannesburg, by London-bred Ghanaian "celebritecht" David Adjaye

"I think it will be a double take with a lot of people, because you will look at this building and think that it is in some other city, and then you will realise its in Johannesburg; it's in Africa," he said. The aim is to "combine an African aesthetic with a contemporary vision."

But why do "African" and "contemporary" have to be incommensurate? Why (and to whom) is it appealing to think you are in another city besides the one, in Africa, that you are in?

An hour later, when the sun was setting pink along the palm tree skyline, a taxi pulled up in front of our grandfather's house and took us downtown, to the new part of Johannesburg swept up and made trendy by a succession of developers and moneyed artists.

We were let out in front of a club with a line of anxious and bored-looking people and let right inside by a bouncer who smiled at Lyndall.

"Thank you, baby." Lyndall reached up and patted the bouncer on top of his bald head. He grabbed for her arm, but she kept walking inside.

By the bar, Lyndall adjusted her top so that her small breasts, boosted to high heaven, erupted from her cowl-neck blouse. Within minutes, we were showered with free drinks. We accepted all of them; we danced with no one. Lyndall, halfway through the night, climbed atop a cocktail table and moved uninhibitedly, throwing her arms in the air, bending at the waist, and shaking her full mane of hair. It was the only moment when she was visibly having fun—the rest of the night seemed like a string of transactions.

A man approached me. He was from Zambia and staying in Joburg to study law at the university. He had a head full of locs that looked neat and freshly twisted. He wore wire-framed glasses and a collared shirt, and looked more like he was going to the office than to a nightclub. His friends were messily hitting on dancing women, but he was reserved and polite, biding his time by the bar. He smelled like cocoa butter. He had a kind smile, and I recognized, for the first time in a while, that I was interested.

We traded conversation, standing next to each other for a good long time.

"You're with her?" He pointed to my cousin, flailing sexily on top of the table.

"She's my cousin." I smiled puzzlingly at him.

"Come home with me." He leaned into me, putting a hand around my waist just as I felt Lyndall tugging at me from the other direction.

"It's time for part two," she said as she pulled me out of the club behind two men in stylish, slim-cut clothing. She led me out to a taxi and then to a hotel. From the modern, marble lobby up to the twentieth floor, to a hotel room laid with designer shopping bags, watches, electronic gadgets left about that suggested the carelessness of wealth. Lyndall could always smell money, even in the dark, in the midst of a crowded nightclub.

The room began to spin. I scarcely registered the number of drinks I'd had because they were all free, handed to me like candy. Both men had short dreads. One sported a leather bowler hat. The other wore thick-rimmed glasses.

The boy with the hat put one arm around my cousin. The other took a seat next to the bed, his lean shoulders hunched away from me, cutting three lines of different-colored powder on the dining table.

"Coca-Cola; my best friend, Tik Tik; and her cousin Special K."

"Aye, I don't fuck with your best friend anymore," Lyndall said. She walked over and hoovered up the white line.

Her head lolled back, she sniffed, and then she laughed deeply. Too drunk to sit up, I watched her from the hotel bed.

"You should have some," she said. "It'll perk you up."

I licked my finger and dabbed some of the coke on my teeth.

Soon, I was wired, telling stupid jokes, singing to the Kwaito music the boys had put on their iPod speakers. The musicians were them. Apparently they were here for a gig and radio spot. They were famous.

"It's boss, yeah?"

"No," I said, and flopped back down on the bed.

"She's not used to such strong stuff," Lyndall said.

I saw her take the boy with the hat by the hand and lead him into the bathroom. I heard her heels click on the bathroom linoleum, the boy's voice echoing from behind the door, then Lyndall's laugh, tinkling like rocks in a glass.

I felt the boy without the hat stick his tongue in my mouth. He darted it around like he was searching for something, his hands riffling through my clothing, over my breasts, under my pants . . . *Oh god, is this really happening?* I heard voices from the bathroom laughing, distracted, ecstatic. I was so drunk, I had to tell myself what was going on. I was being kissed, groped, aggressively and unwanted. I told myself to kiss back. I don't know why.

"Wait!" I pulled away from the boy. I was too scared to tell him to stop. If he was capable of doing this, he was capable of anything.

"What?"

"Is there somewhere else we can go?"

"No."

He took his penis out of his pants. It was semihard. He rubbed it furiously in his right hand and started groaning. *Oh god, oh god, oh god.*

Just then we heard the bathroom door unlatch, and Lyndall's voice.

"You're so naughty, I can tell!"

He stuffed it back in his pants, then covered his crotch with the tail of his shirt.

"What are you getting up to?" Lyndall's voice was unnervingly high. I ran over to her, grabbed her by the hand, and ran out of the room. At the front desk, we called a cab.

As we flew along the highway back toward the suburbs, only lit-up billboards and the distant lights of the city were visible. I thought about how similar Johannesburg looked to where I lived. Save for the occasional pedestrian walking on the side of the highway, we could have been in New York or Los Angeles. I thought about how every place on Earth contained its tragedies, love stories, people surviving and others falling, and for this reason, from far enough of a distance and under enough darkness, they were all essentially the same.

Winnie Mandela bore a strong physical resemblance to my mother: They had the same complexion, same nose, same warm, unassuming smile. When I first heard the accusations against Mrs. Mandela, I weighed the brutality of the charges against her physical appearance. She could appear stern sometimes, as my mother could—no-nonsense, the kind of woman you wouldn't want to encounter after sneaking home past curfew. But the dissonance between what she represented to the country (her nickname is "Mother of the Nation") and what she is alleged to have done is almost impossible to reconcile.

Almost impossible to reconcile if you believe that motherhood and brutality are diametrically opposed. The truth is that motherhood is stained with blood, tainted with suffering and the potential for tragedy. Why are we surprised when a mother—a real mother, someone who takes care of her children and loves them—commits atrocious crimes? These are questions I wrestle with in the days and weeks that I consider my own pregnancy.

Zinzi Clemmons

From the Truth and Reconciliation Commission of South Africa's report, volume two

The Mandela United Football Club (MUFC) was the source of considerable violence and controversy between 1987 and 1989. Whilst Ms Madikizela-Mandela denied this, both the liberation movement externally and the MDM [Mass Democratic Movement] internally recognized it and stated so clearly in their statements of 16 February 1989. In the face of criticism and concerns raised by senior leaders of the liberation movement both at home and in exile, as well as the outrage of the local community, it is difficult to understand why she failed to recognise the threat that the club was posing and how damaging this was to herself. Her reluctance to disband the club is inexplicable.

Ms Madikizela-Mandela denied in her testimony that there was a close relationship between her and the youths who lived on or frequented her property. However, the testimony of former MUFC members, and of individuals who tried to dissuade her from this association, indicates that Madikizela-Mandela took a much more active interest than she has admitted. The MDM statement affirms this: Not only is Mrs Mandela associated with the team, in fact the team is her own creation.

The effects of racial and economic oppression figure largely in the structure and functioning of Black families. Black women play integral roles in the family and frequently it is immaterial whether they are biological mothers, sisters, or members of the extended family. From the standpoint of many Black daughters it could be: my sister, my mother; my aunt, my mother; my grandmother, my mother. They are daughters all and they frequently "mother" their sisters, nieces, nephews, or cousins as well as their own children.

Mr Sono testified that on Sunday 13 November, Mr Michael Siyakamela, Ms Madikizela-Mandela's temporary driver, came to his house. He was told that someone wanted to see him. When he went out, he saw Lolo sitting in the back of the minibus, with Madikizela-Mandela in the front seat. Lolo's face was swollen and bruised. Sono testified that Madikizela-Mandela informed him that Lolo was a police spy and that the MK cadres at Jerry Richardson's house had been killed because of him. Despite his pleas to Madikizela-Mandela to release his son, Lolo was taken away. Madikizela-Mandela allegedly told him: "I am taking this dog away. The movement will see what to do to him."

This was the last time that Mr Sono saw his son.

Ms Madikizela-Mandela has denied any knowledge of or involvement in the abductions, assaults and killing of Lolo Sono or Sibuniso Tshabalala.

In this regard I find myself dubious about the politics of women's peace groups, for example, which celebrate maternality as the basis for engaging in antimilitarist work. I do not see the mother with her child as either more morally credible or more morally capable than any other woman. A child can be used as a symbolic credential, a sentimental object, a badge of self-righteousness. I question the implicit belief that only "mothers" with "children of their own" have a real stake in the future of humanity.

On 29 December 1989, four youths—Pelo Mekgwe, Thabiso Mono, Kenneth Kgase and Moeketsi Stompie Seipei—were abducted from the Methodist manse in Soweto and taken to the Mandela home in Diepkloof Extension. The youths were accused of engaging in sexual relations with the Reverend Paul Verryn, the priest who ran the manse, and Seipei was singled out and accused of being a police informer. All four youths were assaulted, Seipei severely.

In early January, Seipei's decomposing body was found in a river-bed on the outskirts of Soweto. His body and head were riddled with injuries and he had been stabbed in the neck three times.

For two weeks in early January, senior religious and community leaders negotiated with Ms Madikizela-Mandela to secure the release of the other youths held at the house. Madikizela-Mandela denied that they were being held against their will and stated that she had rescued them from sexual abuse at the manse.

When the youths were eventually released and the story spread to the media, Madikizela-Mandela issued several statements and conducted interviews in which she attacked the church for orchestrating a massive cover-up. The war of words continued into February. Following the identification of Stompie Seipei's body, several members of the MUFC, including Mr Jerry Richardson, were arrested and charged with murder.

Ms Madikizela-Mandela has denied any knowledge of or involvement in the killing of Stompie Seipei on 1 January 1989.

The Commission received three versions of this killing. Jerry Richardson, who was convicted for the murder and applied for amnesty, claimed that he killed Seipei on Madikizela-Mandela's instructions. Katiza Cebekhulu claimed that he witnessed Madikizela-Mandela stabbing Stompie Seipei, a version supported by John Morgan, who testified that he was instructed to dump Seipei's body. The third version was presented in the form of an unsigned, typed section 29 detention statement from Mr Johannes 'Themba' Mabotha, a Vlakplaas askari who frequented the Mandela home, which states that he was present at a meeting when Richardson informed Madikizela-Mandela that he had killed Seipei. Although this statement claims that Madikizela-Mandela was shocked at what Richardson had told her, it goes on to allege that she was directly involved in an attempt to spread misinformation that Seipei was alive and had been seen in a refugee camp in Botswana. A further version, suggested by former Security Branch policeman Paul Erasmus, is that Richardson killed Seipei because he (Seipei) had found out that Richardson was an informer.

The various versions, with the exception of that of Erasmus, all implicate Ms Madikizela-Mandela, either directly or indirectly, in Seipei's murder or its attempted cover-up.

On my last Christmas with my mother, we were in South Africa, where we ate dinner at my grandfather's house in Johannesburg. We had slipped out of Philadelphia just before a snowstorm hit, while summer reigned in Joburg. I spent the morning doing laps in the pool at our vacation house and the evening in a Santa hat, eating beef tongue and fish biryani.

We sat in my grandfather's living room, scraping the last bits of trifle from our dessert plates. A soccer game played on the TV. My aunts and uncles, cousins and second cousins were all there. Conversation turned to my grandmother, my mother's mother and matriarch of the family. It had been some time since she died—I was still in junior high when she passed away—but our family dinners were still marked by her absence.

"Aish," my mother said into her trifle, "the worst times are when I wake up and I think, 'I have to call Mama to say hello.'"

I realized that that was how heartbreak occurred. Your heart wants something, but reality resists it. Death is inert and heavy, and it has no relation to your heart's desires.

Before everyone went home, the family gathered for a prayer of departure. My grandfather thanked God for all the family that had come from near and far. He asked God for our safe flight back home. And then he asked—his voice breaking—

to heal my mother, and in response there were mumbled yeses, hallelujahs from around the room.

We said our goodbyes and loaded into the car. It was dark by then. My father was driving, my mother in the passenger seat. I sat in the back, cradling a tinfoil-topped ceramic dish full of tepid curry. I held it on my lap, letting it warm the tops of my thighs. The weather was hot during the day, but cold as late autumn at night.

We were driving on the N1 for less than ten minutes when we saw brake lights multiply in front of us. There was a traffic jam up ahead. Then there was the flashing red and yellow of emergency vehicles. An ambulance and police car were parked on the shoulder, outside the driver's side of the car. An officer and two ambulance workers stood between the two emergency vehicles, their heads pointed at the ground before them.

I knew what it was before I even saw anything. My family had told us of the daily accidents on that road, of the day laborers who crossed the many lanes to get from one side to the other and were often clipped by flying cars. I heard my mother's gasp from the front seat, but it was more than that. There was the knowledge, heavy on my heart, that something was very wrong. As we got closer to the scene, I made out the dead body of a man on the ground before the workers. He was lying faceup, his torso minced horizontally into three pieces.

"Must've been walking on the highway," my father said, clucking solemnly.

"Shame," my mother whimpered in return.

I couldn't speak; I could only shudder. My stomach turned,

but I could not look away. I craned my neck all the way around as we crawled past the scene, until I could no longer see the man through the back windshield. Traffic picked up and we turned off the highway, up the hill, and into the driveway of our vacation home. The man was still on my mind, but he was fading. I still felt a small tinge of horror, I felt a bit less safe. I felt sad for him, for any family he might have had. But there was not much time to think of him as we unloaded our dishes and bags and gifts from the car. I had to carry all my things, including the precarious curry dish, in one hand.

My other arm I offered to my mother, and she leaned heavily on it up the stone walkway to our front door. She was shaky and tired from the long day. It took us many minutes, and many times I was afraid I would drop something or that she would fall, but eventually, we reached the front door, and we all went to sleep peacefully that night, grateful for the life that we still had.

She's gone.

But she's here, I can feel her. I can see her that day they told us that everything was going to be all right.

But she's not here.

But I can feel her arms around me. It feels like the breeze coming off the river. It enwraps me with its warmth. It comforts me. It smells like her breath.

But she's long gone.

But maybe I can be happy with something else. If I feel happy and shut my eyes, maybe it will be the same.

But it will never be the same.

PART THREE

When Peter is gone, my body enters a period of slow motion from which I cannot emerge. Everything moves underwater. My body feels already extremely pregnant, as does my mind. There is little difference between week two and week eight.

Our heroes tend to be orphans. Beowulf, Batman, even Harry Potter. There are plenty of plausible explanations. Perhaps they all began as spectacular individuals, and not having parents afforded them more room to define their identity in a spectacular way? Or does the loss of parents endow them with a drive to do greater things? Do they just have more to prove? Or do we simply view the loss of parents as the most tragic of situations, so that a person who overcomes such a circumstance is necessarily imbued with some aspect of heroism?

Arguably South Africa's greatest hero, Nelson Mandela wrote in his autobiography of feeling "cut adrift" after his father's death. It was the experience that led him to leave his childhood home, thus signaling a literal and figurative departure from childhood:

Late that night he called for Nodayimani, "Bring me my tobacco," he told her. My mother and Nodayimani conferred and decided that it was unwise that he have tobacco in his current state. But he persisted in calling for it, and eventually Nodayimani filled his pipe, lit it, and then handed it to him. My father smoked and became calm. He continued smoking for perhaps an hour, and then, his pipe still lit, he died.

I do not remember experiencing great grief so much as feeling cut adrift. Although my mother was the center of my existence, I defined myself through my father. My father's passing changed my whole life in a way that I did not suspect at the time. After a brief period of mourning, my mother informed me that I would be leaving Qunu. I did not ask her why, or where I was going.

I packed the few things that I possessed, and early one morning we set out on a journey westward to my new residence. I mourned less for my father than for the world I was leaving behind. Qunu was all that I knew, and I loved it in the unconditional way that a child loves his first home. Before we disappeared behind the hills, I turned and looked for what I imagined was the last time at my village. I could see the simple huts and the people going about their chores; the stream where I had splashed and played with the other boys; the maize fields and green pastures where the herds and flocks were lazily grazing. I imagined my friends out hunting for small birds, drinking the sweet milk from the cow's udder, cavorting in the pond at the end of the stream. Above all else, my eyes rested on the three simple huts where I had enjoyed my mother's love and protection. It was these three huts that I associated with all my happiness, with life itself, and I rued the fact that I had not kissed each of them before I left. I could not imagine that the future I was walking toward could compare in any way with the past that I was leaving behind.

The cliché that is uttered by survivors of the dead, especially children who have lost beloved parents, is that the child or survivor wants to make them proud. I'm doing this for Dad, they will say and point to the sky, while ascending a mountain or giving a virtuoso performance to an adulatory crowd. And there is always the single tear, reminding us of both the pain and the glory of success, both perfectly present in that single, clean display of emotion. This is how it is supposed to work, to remind us that the universe is perfectly in balance, and those who suffer will be rewarded with triumph.

This thought was foremost in my mind when watching Obama's victory speech in Grant Park in 2008. The Obama family—so sharply dressed in black and bright red, which contrasted with their glowing brown skin—looked literally new, with their fresh hairstyles and vibrant clothing. They were also something we Americans had never seen before. They—a young, handsome black family, installed as our nation's figureheads, buoyed by the support of millions—were new to us, as a nation.

Their four small figures cut against the expansive stage and American flags behind them as well as the huge park itself. The thousands of supporters below them were seen wildly celebrating as heard in their cheers and the flashbulbs that popped at us from the TV screen.

From the negative space above and around the new first family, one could infer the presence of the departed, of all those who had made this day possible. I imagined Obama's ancestors, and freedom fighters, civil rights leaders, Martin Luther King Jr., Malcolm X, even Jesse Jackson—those whose names we knew through history—and Obama's own father, a specter of fear and incomprehensibility for many.

And then there is Ann Dunham, who planted so many seeds, but died before she could see any more than the faintest green hint of his promise. One imagines her looking on from whatever heaven she's chosen, utterly surprised, satisfied beyond comprehension. This is the orphan's ultimate fantasy.

I think sometimes that had I known [my mother] would not survive her illness, I might have written a different book—less a meditation on the absent parent, more a celebration of the one who was the single constant in my life. In my daughters I see her every day, her joy, her capacity for wonder. I won't try to describe how deeply I mourn her passing still. I know that she was the kindest, most generous spirit I have ever known, and that what is best in me I owe to her.

This passage comes from the preface to the 2004 edition of *Dreams from My Father,* which contextualizes the book nine years after its original publication in 1995. Obama had secured a book deal following his history-making election as the first African American president of the *Harvard Law Review*. A few months after the book's publication, Obama's mother passed away from cancer. The year 1996 marked his official entrance into politics after he was elected to the Illinois State Senate.

My leave from university meant that when I returned, the few friends I'd made were gone. Thankfully, that included Dean and his new girlfriend, who, I heard through the grapevine, had moved to a loft in Brooklyn and started a band together. I had taken classes at a college in Philadelphia to keep up, but still graduated a year late.

I studied politics and philosophy, and graduated cum laude. Aminah, Frank, and my father showed up at my graduation. Aminah was her usual overbearing self, snapping countless photos and asking me to pose with her in front of ivy-covered buildings and rusting statues. My father was proud but distracted.

In order to pay my bills, I had to dip into my inheritance account, and every time I withdrew, I said it would be my last, or that I would slow my spending, but gradually, the money was eaten away as if by the cancer that killed her. By graduation, half of my inheritance was gone. It devastated me to think that she worked so hard to save that money, and that I spent it so easily.

The night of commencement, we had dinner at the Mediterranean restaurant at the bottom of College Hill. The place was filled with other cap-and-gown graduates clutching balloons and flowers. Aminah inspected them.

"That girl is so beautiful," she said of one student I'd seen around campus. "Could they be any louder?" she said of a group of boys. I could offer no comment on any of them—I knew not a one.

I took a job in New York, at a government agency that dealt with AIDS research. I found an apartment in Harlem, in an old brownstone on the same block where James Baldwin once lived. My job paid for me to take classes toward a master's in public health at Columbia University, so usually I was busy nights and weekends. My father and Aminah visited me from Philadelphia sometimes, and they took me for the only nice dinners I ate.

Aminah moved back to Philadelphia after graduating from NYU. Frank found a job at UBS, and they bought a duplex apartment not far from Rittenhouse Square. Their wedding was on the grounds of the college in our hometown, where I was a reluctant maid of honor in an awkward one-sleeved dress.

Frank's brother walked me down the aisle. Aminah wore a figure-hugging sheath, and when I saw her in the dressing room all done up, I felt for the first time what breathtaking meant. I couldn't help but get emotional, even though it—the white dress with the five-figure price tag—was not something I believed in. It was also something I knew I would never have, because the only person who would have forced such a ceremony on me was gone.

After the ceremony, Frank's brother hit on me relentlessly. Formerly the awkward geek, I had morphed into something he now found appealing. He whispered in my ear something so saccharine it made me blush, but I did it for the hell of it. Thirteen-year-old me was applauding from the bleachers. When nearly everyone had gone home, I followed him to his childhood bedroom, imagining that I was Aminah—sixteen, gorgeous, and a daring guest in that stately old home. The next morning, I watched Frank's brother sleep for ten minutes. His hair was thinner, age rounding out his features—a shadow of his teenage self. I felt myself wanting more.

I have yearned for certain sensations—the feeling of being able to contain someone's hopes and fears in one touch. I have longed for it with Peter, although at other times with him I have felt it.

Over the phone the next few weeks, Peter and I begin to think about how we will share our child. In my mind, I think that this is betting on a lot. It is so wishful of us to plan, that first this child will be born, that I won't die in labor or kill it by dropping it on its head. There are endless ways this child can die, and they are all the result of my possible mistakes.

I somehow manage to go to work, to come home at night and fix my dinner, and, regardless of how little I've slept, wake myself the next morning, dress, and get to work on time. In the beginning, I tell Aminah nothing, but then, when we are speaking on the phone one day, she asks why I haven't said Peter's name in weeks. I tell her about his last weekend in Brooklyn, how cold and distant he suddenly became, how he couldn't wait to get on that plane. It doesn't make sense to her, how the change could have happened so suddenly—from being in love to no longer speaking. I tell her that he is different, that he cares for me, that he won't be one of those who just disappears. I wield excuse after excuse and none of them work. I have to admit to her the truth—about the baby still growing inside me that is Peter's.

My father is less and less available. When I call him, he answers the phone in a low voice and hurries me off the line. As he is hanging up the phone, I swear I hear a woman's voice on the other end. Sometimes I call his number and just cry into his voicemail. I ask if he can visit me in New York, but he says that he is busy, always busy. *You never had so many plans before,* I tell him. *You're being very emotional,* he says, stressing the last word as if it is an uncomfortable sweater he is being forced to wear. I envy the flatness in his voice, the feeling that he has steadily moved uphill away from our tragedy while I have managed to slide myself back down into a pit.

Why, why, why? Aminah prods me with this word over and over, and I have no answer. I have done only what I could manage. I have had no strength to terminate the baby, or to handle an adoption; I have only persisted, and it has landed me at this point. When I tell her how far along I am, she sighs heavily. She knows what I have been hiding from myself the past few weeks. The baby is a baby now. There's no way to deal with this easily. I can still give it up for adoption, she tells me hopefully, but this option seems the least likely. I can't imagine carrying the baby to term only to give it away. The shame of having to admit to the world that I can't care for the baby seems unbearable.

I feel like I am walking on land again, like my effort is getting me somewhere.

I call on a Sunday and he again tries to hurry me off the phone.

I have no time for formalities. "What's her name?" I demand of him, and he tells me.

The woman's name is Elma. They have been seeing each other for the past three months, he says. It's nothing serious *yet,* he is careful to mention. She is a secretary in the admissions office at the college. After he tells me this, I am silent for a while on the phone, letting myself marinate in bitterness.

"I didn't know how to tell you, so I didn't say anything. I didn't know what to do. Thandi, are you there?"

"I am."

"I want to be happy again," he says, his voice breaking. "Don't you think I deserve happiness?"

"Of course," I say. "You deserve much more than that. I only wish I could be okay with what form of happiness you've chosen."

"Well, you know, these things choose us."

"Hmmph," I grunt. "Well, I don't want to meet her. I don't want to know her. Do you hear me?"

"Yes, honey, that's fine. I understand."

I can't stop repeating it in my head: Elma. Elma. Elma. I have the sudden urge to stab something.

"Dad, I'm pregnant."

The spare room in Aminah and Frank's townhouse is outfitted in antique floral prints, medals and trophies from Frank's high school days, and pictures of Aminah's father. The effect is a strange mash-up of WASP-Afrocentric style that I am forced to take in every night.

Aminah has accosted me into staying with her and Frank for a week. On the phone one day, she suggests gently, then more forcefully, that I could use some time to rest.

"I can rest well enough in my own apartment."

"It will be good for you to be around friends."

I run out of excuses with Aminah, so I call in at work, lying to my boss that I have the flu. My boss is satisfied with this explanation for my recent erratic behavior. I pack my bag and take a train to Philadelphia.

For dinner, Aminah cooks me meals composed mostly of vegetables from the farmer's market—no risky foods like seafood or rare meat. At the dinner table, she and Frank have wine from the wine fridge that glows like a spaceship under their new countertops. She's bought me nonalcoholic wine, but I refuse that.

"I can have up to a glass a day. They say it's even good for you."

But Aminah just dips her head. She is doing her standard steel gaze—she pretends she hasn't heard me.

"Asparagus?" she holds a gold-rimmed platter out to me.

Later that night, Aminah buries me under stacks of blankets.

"I feel like a real pregnant woman," I say. "You got me all laid up here. I'm not on bed rest, you know."

She does her steel gaze again and leaves the room. After she's gone I try to decide exactly what I've done to offend her—is it the pregnancy itself, or the fact that I don't seem to be taking it as seriously as she thinks I should?

Frank works from home the third day. In the morning he cooks me scrambled eggs; he peels and sections my orange, slices my apples into eighths with the cores cut out.

"Peanut butter?" he offers.

"No," I say.

Frank has filled out since high school; I notice white hairs where there was only jet black, pushed perfectly back on his head. I can see in his eyes how his long days have begun to wear on him. I also see what Aminah has always seen in him. He has that same thing that my father has—that only some men do—that extra bit of wiring that makes them stay.

"Aminah's being tough on you 'cause she cares," he says. "That's her way."

"I know," I say. He gives me the best reply that he can give, which is to not require anything of me at all. For a while, we sit there at the table in silence, slightly older and fatter than our high school selves, only slightly closer to each other. Then he takes my plate, carries it to the sink and cleans it, and lets me wander back to my room, to carry on with my day as I please.

My mother's pain was her second disease. It was constant, bracing. At first, she kept it contained with a twenty-milligram OxyContin, taken three times daily. She had a travel alarm clock that she carried with her in her handbag, which she set every morning, then reset for four hours later when it went off. Her purse was a mess of prescription bottles and paraphernalia, including crackers for the medicines she had to take with food, smelling salts for the ones that knocked her out, Pepto-Bismol for the ones that made her nauseated. She managed the routine well, with the duty and spirit befitting someone of her profession.

The pain she experienced from disease is unimaginable. This is not an empty statement, a flaccid grasp at empathy. Chronic pain is one of the most difficult states for humans not suffering from it to imagine. That is because most of us experience pain only for moments, or, maximum, for a few days during an extended stay at the hospital, and even then it is not constant. Few of us will experience the level of pain that does not respond to powerful painkillers. That is a hell reserved for the very unlucky.

When you have chronic pain, the feeling that most people experience only in peaks becomes your baseline. Its effects are similar to those of the drugs that are often used to treat it. It is mood altering, causing changes in personality and even hallucinations. Pain can be a disease in itself.

We stopped fighting as much. She stopped screaming. Her touch became lighter. She had more patience, and physically, she actually felt lighter.

In time, her pain outgrew the medication. It became too much for the one or two pills and polite rituals she was so adept at managing. Her dose grew to forty milligrams, to sixty, eventually to two hundred milligrams of OxyContin three times per day. This was just for maintenance, so that my mother wouldn't go into withdrawal coming off the medicine. Several times a day the pain came on fast and quick, and she'd be immobilized, crying and begging for me or my father to do something. When this happened, we gave her more oxycodone on top of her regular dose. Sometimes it helped. But help never meant that the pain was gone, only that it was lessened.

When the pills weren't enough anymore, her doctor put my mother on a morphine drip. She started sleeping more hours than she was awake, and she couldn't tell us that she was hurting anymore. All we could do was guess if she was suffering by the depth and frequency of her breaths, by the restlessness of her limbs. And then, all we could do was push a button on a little machine, releasing a tiny burst of medicine, and hope that it helped her.

She lost weight. She went from a size 14 to a 12, to a 10, and then to my size, a healthy 6, before she was bedridden and we stopped counting. She was weaker, her skin more prone to bruising, her bones more fragile. She needed support whenever she walked, and I would often offer it in the form of an elbow or a shoulder. Toward the end of her life, I could lift her entire weight into her wheelchair.

Peter calls me to explain his absence. He was terrified, he says, once he actually started to think about what raising a child would entail. He could only see it failing.

"That sounds like a lie, I know," he says, and chuckles a little nervously when I don't answer right away. I make a mental note never to tell Aminah this.

We talk for an hour. That night, I sleep better than I have in years. He is the one with whom I share this burden, and when he is back, I feel less alone with it. But when I wake up, I remember my situation. I caress my stomach. Somehow, in these past few weeks, I have become more tender toward it. Barely awake in bed, I look down at it and begin to cry. But then I get out of bed. I wash, I dress, and I leave for work, the weight of my body feeling so hot, so unstable, like it is about to explode.

Love is also like this. I make one of those infernal lists that every best friend and romantic comedy suggests making during periods of amorous decision-making, where I enter the pros and cons of a relationship with Peter. These are the results:

Intelligent	I think I'm smarter than he is
Curious	He doesn't challenge me
He makes me feel deeply at ease	Hasn't figured out his life yet
He takes care of me	Was hesitant about becoming a father (dad issues??)
Will make a good father	Lacks a certain joie de vivre
Stable	Not conventionally handsome
Cute	We don't have *great* sex anymore
We have good sex (regular, consistent)	I know he will never leave me
He will never leave me	

This always occurs, no matter how reckless the people involved. I fall in love carefully.

We winnow one person out of all those we meet and deem sexually attractive and worth several hours of our time. We get to know each other. We decide, against all better judgment, to take on the risk and pair with this person. We like someone. They like us; we stay together, we fuck our brains out, like turns to love. We ignore all the little nuisances of their personalities.

Then trouble intrudes. For some, the relationship flares into violence. Some simply fade out and stop calling; they fall into someone else's bed. You splinter and you split.

We want to be together. We want to stay. This is our default setting.

We love each other. We are having a baby together. The choices are few, and there is a clearly logical one.

Peter and I marry on a spring day on a Pennsylvania mushroom farm, half an hour west of where I grew up. His mother and father fly in from Portland, along with college friends from California, Hawaii, and Spain.

I allow my father to bring his girlfriend.

Aminah is the only one accompanying me to the altar; I won't bow to the pressures of tradition and be traded between two men. I wear an ochre gown that I find in a consignment maternity store. It was a bridesmaid's dress, not a bridal gown. Aminah skins up her face the first time she sees it, but over time, she stops objecting.

I'm so big by this time that I rely on her arm for support. I'm so pregnant I feel dizzy.

Peter looks giddy as I walk down the aisle. I feel swollen and odd. The sun turns his red hair translucent, his suit slightly too large around his shoulders. But there is nothing about him I would change.

Peter's cousin officiates, and he says only a few words, and then we kiss; we rush out of there, for it's time to eat. We hurry back down the aisle the way we came, except this time our hands are joined in the air like we've just won a game. It's all joy and celebration, and fast, without hitches—barely time for a pause, just as I designed. There's no time to cry for who isn't there.

We name our son Mahpee, after the sky. Our friends and family chide us for the name, and we are embarrassed for how odd and romantic it is, but we don't take it back. We do shorten it to M. His real name is a keepsake between the two of us.

M has my button nose and Peter's freckles. His hair starts off smooth and amber colored when he is born, and then falls out, grows back in rough, kinky, and mahogany colored, with flecks of gold sprinkled throughout. If we created a scale between me and Peter, M would be halfway between. There is no way I can look at him without seeing Peter.

Peter and I are happy, and M is too. He is always smiling, even when he is sleeping, and even when he's fussy, he just kicks his fat little legs, that permanent smile still etched on his pink lips. We can't stay mad at him. When we're tired, we grow angry at each other. *You made him cry. You made him angry. You fed him too much and made his poop green!*

My father learns quickly to be a grandfather. Aminah and Frank threaten to put off their baby-making indefinitely, they are so preoccupied as aunt and uncle. Peter had a hard time leaving Portland, but he likes New York enough. I drain the rest of the money out of my mother's inheritance and buy us a small, plastic-sided house with a small yard way out in the farther reaches of Queens. The house is musty and the walls are thin, but there's enough space for all of us without feeling cramped—extremely rare in New York City. Some days, we're even able to forget how far we are from friends and amusements (what we formerly conceived of as "civilization"), how draining our commutes are. On hard days, we want to leave, but on good days, we feel like we have everything we need.

M sits between us. His favorite move is to link Peter's fingers in mine, and then, giggling mischievously, crawl behind one of our legs and hide. He does this especially when Peter and I are fighting or distant. There is something about him—he has a sense for knowing which spaces to fill in people. Even if it never helps him on a test or in a game, I will always be proud of him for this.

Every time I touch him I think, how can something be this soft? It is impossible, this feeling of his newness against my coarse fingers. His every bone and skin cell is in a state of formation. He is coming into being before my eyes.

I have also felt sublime terror since he was born. It is impossible to think of him without thinking of his death—when he falls from the couch, when I struggle to hold him after a long day. I imagine him falling from a great height, the terrible sound, the way his body will become foreign with the life gone. I have never wanted someone as much as him and simultaneously been so afraid of that person being taken away.

Aminah's father has a heart attack. It is his second; the first was three years ago, and he recovered fairly quickly then. This time, though, he is older, weaker. His doctors order him to walk slower, and he has to hook up to an oxygen machine when he is at home.

He starts to recover, to walk around the neighborhood without help, and eventually he drives into the city to visit my father. They go back to watching football again at their favorite bar on Sundays, though he stops short of the Eagles parking lot, which would mean disaster.

Aminah tells me he confided in her that he was shocked by my mother's death, brought down, and I realize that I've noticed a certain light gone from his eyes. He isn't funny in the wild way that he used to be, telling rude jokes in all manner of company. He is a softer, more quiet man since he saw her go—as we all are—sobered, constitutionally, by the experience.

Then one day, he has another heart attack. It isn't a large one, but it is enough to push him over the edge. He dies quickly, before he is able to feel much pain, in a manner totally opposite from my mother's death. Aminah calls me crying from the hospital and I take the bus down to Philadelphia a few hours later to be with her. We are part of the same grim club.

I begin to feel a mortal disadvantage. Aminah and I are well-off. We both come from the same neighborhood. Our loved ones aren't likely to die unexpectedly from gun violence, or to perish from diabetes or obesity, those side effects of poverty with which we are familiar. We never became accustomed to worrying that, because of where we lived, like that postal worker on the television, one of our loved ones would go out one day and not come home.

But the numbers are what they are: Out of all the people my age whom I know, one white friend has lost a parent. Out of Aminah's friends, who are mostly black, four. Aminah is my closest black friend, and each of us has lost a parent. After the death of Aminah's father, I begin to awaken to those statistics, knowing them to be more real than they have ever been in the past.

Figure 1. Life expectancy at birth, by race and sex and Hispanic origin: United States, 1980–2008

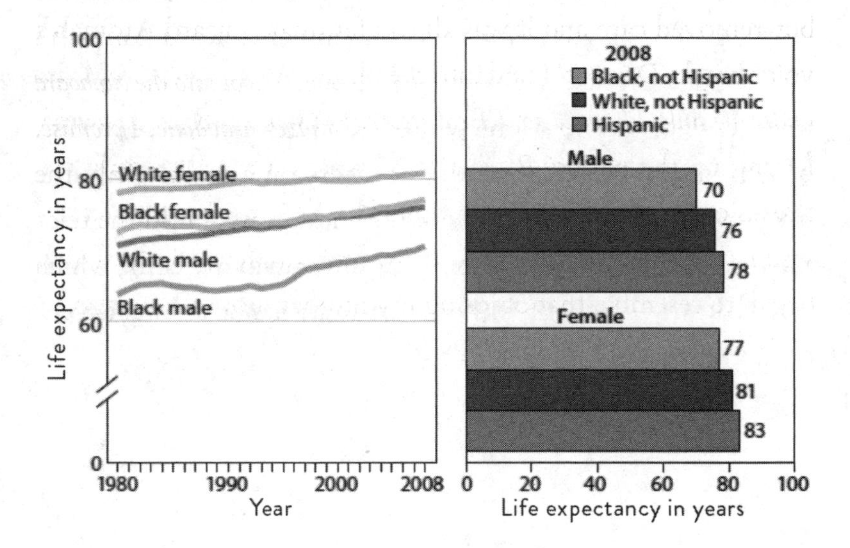

The gap in life expectancy at birth between white persons and black persons persists but has narrowed since 1990.

Life expectancy is a measure often used to gauge the overall health of a population. From 1980 to 2008, life expectancy at birth in the United States increased from 70 years to 76 years for males and from 77 years to 81 years for females. Racial disparities in life expectancy at birth persisted for both males and females in 2008 but had narrowed since 1990. In 2008, Hispanic males and females had longer life expectancy at birth than non-Hispanic white or non-Hispanic black males and females.

SOURCE: CDC/NCHS, *Health, United States, 2011,* **Table 22.** Data from the National Vital Statistics System (NVSS).

As soon as I got the news, I called Aminah. She told me about the hospital, the smells, and the stages and the compassionate-but-removed care and it was all too familiar. I heard Aminah's voice break. *Dammit!* I said into the phone. *M got into the cupboard under the sink. I have to go. I'll call you right when I'm done, I promise.* I hung up the phone. Peter and M were on a walk. Only the television in the living room looked back at me. I told the television that it couldn't possibly know the pain in my belly, which began to resemble that of losing my mother, not so long ago.

Love and marriage are completely unrelated enterprises. Marriage bears as little resemblance to love as competing in the Olympics does to your afternoon jog. Sometimes I think with regret of how our love might have grown if we hadn't driven a pregnancy, then a marriage—like two speeding 18-wheelers—straight into it.

Peter tells me he wants to lose weight. I accuse him of fishing. What he really wants is for me to say that he doesn't need to lose weight. I have noticed the extra ring of skin around his chin, the ring of flesh that hangs over his belt when he bends down. It's like the man I married has been swallowed by another man who seems embarrassed by this fact. I have put on the extra pound or so, but I don't let it change the way I walk, the things I wear. As so many self-help books have said, I wear the fat; it doesn't wear me. I can't bring myself to say that he still looks the same to me. He doesn't. "I still love you," I say, with all the sincerity I can muster.

The next morning, a Sunday, I awaken to the sound of metal on wood; in the backyard, Peter is splitting firewood with the ax that I gave him for Christmas, which had lain unopened for months next to our fireplace. Peter's Blazers sweatshirt is ringed with sweat under the armpits, his hair wet, his brow glinting, the unmistakable look of fury on his face.

Peter wakes me in the middle of the night. His face hangs over me and he is snarling, baby bottle in one hand, M in the other. He's shaken me awake, and from the look on his face, it's taken him a while to do so.

"You take him for fucking once!" he screams as he pulls my hands from under the blankets and wraps the baby in them. I struggle to sit up before the baby can fall. The bottle rolls to the floor and M's head falls out of my grasp. He starts screaming.

"What are you doing?" I scream. "You'll hurt him!"

"He's not made of china," Peter says, sniffing as he lies back down in bed, pulling the covers over his shoulder and switching off his bedside lamp.

I place M on my lap so that he's looking at me and mime some funny faces at him. Soon he stops screaming. I hold him in the air so that his feet bounce on my legs, his favorite game. He starts to coo softly.

"I can't do anything right," I hear Peter grumble from underneath the covers.

I gather M, his bottle, and his blanket, and move to the armchair in the living room, where we watch the sunrise together. Peter snores from the bedroom.

Peter, M, and I attend the funeral of Aminah's father, which is held at the small Episcopalian chapel on the college's campus. The entire administration is there, plus students, and work colleagues of Aminah's mother, and our fathers' mutual friends.

We dress M in little black trousers and a navy blue polo shirt. He wrestles out of his tiny socks and shoes and lies sideways in his carrier during the service, but he doesn't cry and he doesn't fall out, so we leave him there, cooing and smiling like a drunk uncle about to fall out of his chair.

I cry openly, freely, from the third pew of the chapel. I snort and sniffle like a maniac. At first, Peter drapes an arm on my shoulder, but then he just looks at me confused and tends to M. The man next to me offers his handkerchief and a smile. I recognize him as Keith, a friendly boy from our childhood. He is older, with more bulk to his shoulders and legs, but his smile and smooth olive skin are still the same. On my other side, M burps and starts laughing. Peter sighs, reaches for the pacifier, and pops it nervously into M's mouth, as if our child is a bottle of champagne threatening to explode.

At the end of the service, I find Aminah and hold her close. We cry long and hard on each other's shoulders.

"I'm so sorry." I use Keith's handkerchief to wipe my tears from her impeccable black peplum dress.

She laughs. "It's fine."

"At least you don't have to worry about mine," I say. My cotton shift is wrinkled and stained by M's throw-up.

"It's not a problem at all." Aminah rubs my back, and I am unsettled as I realize that she is, even at this moment, the one reassuring me.

That night, as has become our norm, Peter falls asleep in front of the television in the living room, and I in our bed with a book. I dream of Keith, and nothing happens in the dream except that he hugs me, strong and with his whole body, and he whispers in my ear that everything is going to be all right. Just like that, in that soft, buttery voice of his that I heard a million times in the classroom and out on the football field, *You're all right, Thandi, everything's gonna be okay.*

M's first word is "shit," though we will later tell people it is "shoot." He got it from Peter, who curses all the time, while cutting the lawn, while cooking dinner, while changing diapers, and, more than me, while storming out of a room in frustration. He is convinced that he will be fired from his job, but when I suggest he look for something else, he gets angry. It's fine for him to suggest things aren't going well, but for me to voice the obvious is too much for him. I never realized before how much pride he had.

My boss decides that I should be the one to go to a vaccines conference in San Diego. I protest as much as I can, but I'm not in good graces after my maternity leave. Peter insists too that I go, and I know it's because he needs time away from me. I don't want to leave M. I plead with him, but he won't hear it. After the trip is decided and my airline tickets show up in my in-box, I feel a sense of palpable dread.

Peter drives me to the airport with M in the backseat; M screeches the entire way. "Shit!" he cries when we drive over potholes. When we arrive at the airport, Peter zips past the parking lot entrance. "Where are you going?" I ask. I remember when he met me in baggage claim during our first visits, how he seemed so nervous he could fall over. He stops in front of the passenger drop-off, gives me a hurried kiss as the car idles. M starts crying when I kiss him goodbye, sensing correctly that I am leaving him, and Peter comforts our son as I lug my suitcase from the trunk. An elderly skycap takes my bag from me. "That's too big for a lady," he says, smiling. I catch him glancing at my husband in the car, and I grab my bag from him and storm toward the departure gate.

The sun sets as we cross the country. Somewhere over Nevada, I see a full moon descend, and something tugs at me. I recognize I am growing away from Peter, have been for a while, but now the truth stares at me, plain and bare. I've been afraid of being left alone with these feelings.

I check into the hotel at eight Pacific time. As soon as I set my bags down in my room, I call Peter to tell him that I've arrived safely. He puts M up to the phone, but he is tired so he only whimpers. It's nighttime in New York. "I love you," I tell Peter, and after I hang up, I lie down in bed with the TV on for white noise. I doze off, and when I wake at midnight I can't fall back asleep.

Down in the hotel bar, I order a red wine, hoping it will make me drowsy, but it does the opposite. I haven't felt the buzz of alcohol in many months. I want more. I order a dirty martini with top-shelf liquor, and something yellow that comes in a champagne flute. Soon I feel as if I am flying, though I am still sitting on a plastic bar stool, my behind slowly becoming sore.

He is sitting at the opposite end of the bar—tall, with dark eyes and dark skin. Broad shoulders knotted with muscles that make him hunch over the bar top. He is familiar to me, like someone I would have dated years ago. Between my second and third drink, he ends up next to me. I learn he works in one of the faceless buildings in midtown Manhattan, making deals for more money than Peter and I make in a month. I find myself repulsed by the canniness of his lines, but high on the fact that they are being used on me. This hasn't happened in so very long.

When we are walking up the stairs, I tell myself I will only let him walk me to my door. When he asks to use the bathroom, I tell myself I will ask him to leave after he emerges. When he touches me, I tell myself I will not let him kiss me.

He leans over me the same way he leaned over the bar, and I feel excited and terrified at once. He pushes me onto the bed and keeps his fingers wrapped around my throat as he pulls off my clothes. I tell myself that I shouldn't enjoy this, but I do.

Is that it?

All this time, I have been tabulating all Peter's little faults, trying to discern which combination of them has added up to my unhappiness. But could it actually be this one simple thing—that I just need to be fucked?

He spends the night in my room, and it's not until he's left the next morning, and I'm alone, that I'm paralyzed by the thought that what I've done can't possibly stay in this room. This will follow me wherever I go.

An object at rest remains at rest, or continues to move at a constant velocity, unless acted upon by an external force.

By the time I ask Peter to move out for a while, we have not gone a single week without fighting since Mahpee's birth. I wait for one of our two-day armistices when I approach him with the proposition. He is sitting in his white armchair in the living room, reading a magazine, when I sit on the armrest and put my computer on his lap. The ad for the temporary rental is on the screen, a one-bedroom apartment in the next neighborhood.

He bristles at first. I can see the fight welling up inside him, but then he sighs, a weary look spreading over his face. "All right," he says.

We make it through the next week without any major fights. On a Monday morning before leaving for work, in addition to preparing his briefcase and coffee, Peter packs one suitcase and leaves it by the door. He calls me into the living room.

I always loved how he traveled light, how he needed nothing more than two outfits, a toothbrush, and a razor to live in the world. Before he leaves, he squeezes M for a long time. He weeps openly, clutching our son's chubby head to his face.

"Okay," he says as he hands the baby to me. He looks like he's on the high dive, staring into icy water fifty feet below. He gives me one last kiss on the forehead, one last hug, and I fight every instinct telling me to apologize, to get him to stay, just this one last time. But I know what I have to do. He straightens his plaid shirt, blotting the wet spot on his shoulder, and walks out the door.

That evening, after I come home from work and pick M up from the sitter, my mind turns from tonight to two weeks from now, to next month, to years from now. I envision, with resignation, my life as a single parent. I cry without pause, even while recognizing that I have done the right thing. The first three days, I barely sleep between anxiety and M, and I nap sitting up, eyes closed, at my desk, until the minute the clock strikes five and I rush out the door.

My favorite television show involves people implausibly redecorating their friends' houses while they're out for dinner. It's the ridiculous premise that roped me in. The results are often slipshod, the contestants' reactions strained. If one of my friends ever did this to me, I would be furious. It's probably the artificiality of the show that I find so amusing, and of course Peter never appreciated kitsch. Peter never took to irony, detesting hipsters. It was one of the reasons I was attracted to him and, predictably, it is one of the things that now irritates me most about him.

"Why can't you just laugh?" I've told him more times than I can count.

By Thursday, I can scarcely imagine another week like the one that's just passed. I've stopped all pretenses of normality. I put M's crib in the living room. I order Chinese food and eat it straight from the container. I have a glass of wine and turn the TV up so that it tunes out M's gurgling and occasional crying. M sits next to me on the couch, and crawls dangerously close to the edge. I push him back over with my ankle. I watch all three reruns of my show until Mahpee starts to wail, then I feed him and wash his little body in the sink. We both fall asleep in the living room that night, and when I wake up, it's 6:00 a.m. and the TV is still on, blaring an infomercial for a mop that looks like every other mop in stores. It's the first time I've slept through the night in as long as I can remember.

Before long, it's Sunday and time for Peter to take Mahpee. I am more than ready to be relieved of my duties. We decide that we will alternate weeks with him while we are living apart.

After M is gone, along with his mini suitcase full of tiny clothes and bath products and half of his toys, the house is quiet. Snow is melting off tree branches outside and falls to earth with an occasional plop! This is a sound I've come to associate with late winter and the beginning of spring, of emerging from a long, dark, and cold period.

I call a therapist and arrange an appointment. When I walk into the waiting room at her office, I suddenly feel very aware of how disheveled I look. I am wearing Peter's old flannel shirt. Its front pocket has ripped off, and I've been using the sleeve as a handkerchief for the past few days.

The therapist starts with the usual background-gathering, thumbing through the paperwork I filled out in the lobby just minutes before. "No addictions, no psychiatric history. Africa, that's interesting."

"South Africa," I correct her. She looks up from the papers briefly, frowns slightly at me, and lowers her eyes again.

"And you're going through a divorce," she says. "I'm sorry to hear that."

"Yeah, well."

"It's quite a common thing for people who have recently experienced loss to rush into relationships," she says robotically. She looks up at me again, reading my expression.

"Oh," I say. "It's that simple."

The therapist smirks, raises her pen in the air, and turns the page. "Well, I can't say that."

"Of course you can't," I mutter.

It takes the rest of the session for her to review the paperwork. At the end of the session, she shakes my hand and says "I look forward to working with you" in a very businesslike manner before ushering me out the front door.

As soon as I get home, I call Aminah and tell her what the therapist said.

"Can you believe how glib she was?" I ask. "Aren't I paying her for something a bit deeper than that?"

"Well . . ." Aminah trails off.

"Excuse me?"

"Thandi, you know how much I like Peter."

"Yeah?"

"But you guys *did* get married very fast."

"My parents got married after two months."

"But do you really think you would've done it if you hadn't gotten pregnant?"

I've had that exact thought so many times, in the depths of arguments with my husband, in my loneliest moments. I've never actually failed anything in my life; even when I was irresponsible, I still managed to earn decent grades by most standards. But throughout our time together, I've had the uncomfortable feeling that with Peter, I'd somehow done everything wrong.

"You know I love you. Maybe it's worth thinking about."

I pause, look again out the window, where the branches are bare and wet and the sun is now shining with full strength. If not for the frost on the window, it would look like spring.

"Well, not all of us are lucky enough to fall in love with our high school sweetheart, who also happens to be rich."

"I thought we were talking about you, not me."

"I meant what I said, Aminah. Your life has been pretty fucking charmed, all right? You can't exactly identify with what I've been going through . . ."

"Look," Aminah says, breezing past me with her usual resolve, "I know this is really hard, and I wish I could be closer to you right now. Why don't you bring M down for a weekend so that we can watch him, okay? And take it easy, try to get some rest. Thandi?"

"Yeah," I say.

"Everything will be all right, I promise."

I dream that I am in my middle school cafeteria. There is an assembly at which I am supposed to speak. My mother is standing over in the corner, wearing her pajamas, turban, and slippers. She is as thin as she was just before she died. She tries to pull me to the corner to give me advice, but she can't speak. She becomes more frustrated and starts weeping. I try to hug her but I can't get my arms around her. The more I try, the more translucent she becomes. I realize that she is a ghost, a hologram, and eventually she disappears, and I am left with nothing but the feeling of emptiness that I knew so long ago.

Sometimes, my dreams of my mother are pleasant. They are peaceful dreams. In them, I barely register her presence, but her presence is what colors them with warmth and comfort. It is enough to make me still feel warm and nurtured after I wake up.

My father marries Elma, who, I realize with time, is a kind and practical woman. My father sells the house in South Africa. The VW he gives to my mother's brother whose car was totaled in an accident. He says he can't afford to keep it up anymore, but I know it's because his new wife has given him new interests. He retires from his job and they travel to South America together. They send M and me postcards from Brazil, Panama, and Chile. Once in a while, a box wrapped in brown paper and colorful stamps arrives containing a rag doll or sugar candy. My father does his adventuring through women, I realize.

Before their marriage, Elma moved into the apartment in Philadelphia, but curiously all my mother's furniture and knickknacks stayed. In personality and taste, she is a woman far simpler than my mother. I'm sure this was a deliberate choice on my father's part. Most people can handle only one truly difficult woman once in their life. I realize the same is probably true for anyone I date.

At first, the idea of the wedding irks me; I have all kinds of one-sided debates with M where I pose him frustrated existential questions and he answers me with gibberish.

One day, Aminah comes over to visit.

"Isn't this what you want too? Someone to take care of your dad?"

She is right, dousing the flames in my mind. I relax after that.

I notice that she has a wobble to her walk. The small of her belly is kissed with roundness. She smiles when I ask her. "It's true," she tells me. We hug and inform M he will have a cousin soon, and he giggles blissfully. He has no idea what we're talking about.

After this, I take my father's marriage mostly in stride. I am grateful that one of us has a happy ending.

I receive an e-mail from Lyndall:

> We heard about the breakup here, we are all very sorry, eh? It's a good thing Papa isn't alive because he hated divorce so much. I swear, not trying to make you feel worse. Even though we never met in person, Peter sounded great. A real nice guy, but, hate to say it cuz, you could do better. And you will. Come over to SA and I'll find you a real nice chap with the right kind of equipment :) :-o ;) No joking I ain't married but I know it's the key to a happy one. If it wasn't working it means it wasn't working know what I'm sayin!! ;) ;) ;))))
>
> I wasn't going to tell you this but Uncle Bertie and his wife were talking about you at Stasia's christening. They said Peter probably cheated on you because your ass got so fat after the baby blah blah blah, that's why the marriage is over. Can you believe that? I told them, the last time Bertie saw his own dick it was still apartheid. He almost knocked me but it was worth it. I'm so sorry to tell you cuz but you had to know. Can you imagine? He said Peter was only with you for your money,

that's the only reason a white boy would be with a black girl. Shoo, I got so angry, but don't worry cause I stood up for you.

Anyway, give little M a kiss and a high five. Stay STRONG.

Love you LOTS

Xoxo,

~L

Every five, six weeks, I open up an envelope from my father and it contains a hundred-dollar bill or two, sometimes a check for five hundred. When M has the flu and has to go to the hospital, a thousand. But there is never enough money, never enough sleep.

M is an incredibly mischievous child. When he is acting up, when we are in the midst of the action, I would say that he is annoying. He is a pain in the ass. Before, I couldn't bear the thought of him being taken away, but now, in my worst moments, I would gladly hand him over to a kidnapper, a kind, gentle kidnapper who would appear at my door and promise to take excellent care of my son. In my bad moments, I would give him over in a second.

I am able to find a one-and-a-half bedroom in Brooklyn after the breakup. I let Peter keep our old place out of guilt. He leaves the house while I pack my things; he is unable, still, to face me after my betrayal. I miss him; walking through the house, picking my things from his only makes me miss him more. I lose all of my baby weight from not eating. I long to see him, but I accept my excommunication as worthy punishment.

I send him a message one night. It takes me one hour to compose: Been thinking about you. Do you ever miss me? He never replies.

M's room is a little windowless corridor—a section of my room, really—walled off by French doors. I have to walk through his room to get to the bathroom or kitchen, and at night I often tussle with myself over how badly I need to use the bathroom or eat an extra snack. Is it worth waking up the little monster and sacrificing another three hours of sleep? Usually, it is not, and I go to bed with my bladder bursting or stomach grumbling.

But then he looks at a book or the television with an intense curiosity I'm not sure anyone's managed at his age, and I realize there is something in him that is limitless. He regards me in a way no one has ever done before: with complete and utter adoration and wonderment.

Even though oftentimes I am lonely, it also feels right, just him and me together in our little apartment.

When Peter is gone, his absence feels familiar. Yes, there is that dark, terrifying loneliness that scares me, but I am acquainted with fear. If I stay inside it long enough, root my heels in deeper, it doesn't feel scary anymore. It feels like home.

When I am feeling overwhelmed, certain thoughts comfort me. Sometimes I am alone and the wind howls. I am lonely and feel that every day is just too much, that I am going to break. It is my prayer, to myself and the heaven that is in my mind, that looks like my childhood home on a winter's day—a place warm and glowing with love and safety.

Some things have to go away, I tell myself. That is just the way it is.

I say this over and over in my head, until the feeling recedes. I repeat it like a prayer, when I look into M's eyes or when I stand at my mother's grave. Both sites are equally enormous; they terrify me equally but in opposite ways.

We are like bricks in a wall, and a new one cannot fit unless another is taken away.

It comforts me to peace, and M to sleep, this harmony, the idea that for every suffering there is equal and opposite joy. In practice, it is so simple, yet so mystical and infinite.

I am beginning to forget my mother. This is the sad truth. I wish, sometimes, for even a bad dream of her that I used to have. It would be preferable to this absence.

I will always be motherless. One day I will be fatherless. And one day after that, if all goes according to nature's plan, M will be motherless.

I pray that I will never be childless.

She comes to me in snatches—I remember pieces of her laugh, the look she gave when she was upset. Sometimes I sniff the bottle of perfume of hers that I saved, but it doesn't come close to the robustness of her smell. It is her, flattened.

This is what it's really like to lose. It is complete and irreversible.

How pernicious these little things called memories are. They barbed me once, but now that I no longer have many of them, I am devastated.

I nuzzle M the way she used to nuzzle me. I tell him that I love him in Afrikaans, like she used to tell me. *Why you talking funny, Mama?* he asks, and looks even more confused when my tears fall onto his little head.

There could be love again; I can see the places where it might fit in my life. I may be ready to try.

I've amazed myself with how well I've learned to live

around her absence. This void is my constant companion, no matter what I do. Nothing will fill it, and it will never go away.

CREDITS

vii: *The Cancer Journals: Special Edition* by Audre Lord.
20 and 25: "Some Observations on Race and Security in South Africa" by Mats Utas, https://matsutas.wordpress.com.
23: Megan Carter/Corbis Premium Historical/Getty Images
24: Megan Carter/Sygma Premium/Getty Images
32: © 1959 Universal Pictures
66, top: © 2011 Brian Smale; bottom: Bettman/Getty Images
115: © Guillaume Jacquenot
118: *Lessons On the Analytic of the Sublime* by Jean-François Lyotard.
119: Excerpt(s) from *No Death, No Fear: Comforting Wisdom for Life* by Thich Nhat Hanh. Copyright © 2002 by Unified Buddhist Church. Used by permission of Riverhead, an imprint of Penguin Publishing Group, a division of Penguin Random House LLC. All rights reserved.
136: Gideon Mendel/Corbis Premium Historical/Getty Images
139: *Common Differences: Conflicts in Black and White Feminist Perspectives* by Gloria I. Joseph and Jill Lewis.
141: *Of Woman Born: Motherhood as Experience and Institution* by Adrienne Rich.
152–3: Excerpt(s) from *Long Walk to Freedom* by Nelson Mandela. Copyright © 1994, 1995 by Nelson Rolihlahla Mandela. Reprinted by permission of Little, Brown and Company.

ACKNOWLEDGMENTS

I could not have written this book without the support of my friends and family, who helped me find my way through the darkness. My Dad, who taught me about hard work and kindness, and Mark, who makes me laugh and always shows up when he is needed. Mom, I miss you.

André, for teaching me so much about love and art every day.

My Aminahs: Stephanie Pottinger, Rachel Broudy, and Jasmine Alexander.

Karole and Morgan Larsson, for taking me in as a wayward soul in New York, for showing me endless love and support. Kim Quiero, for being a fabulous adopted auntie.

Sue-Chin and Edward Keane, for your love and conversation.

Marcellus Alexander, Glenn Ellis Jr. and Sr., and Janet Lynch.

Lorna, Harris, Josie Welkom, and Yentl Vertuin.

Ron Wilson.

The Broudy family and Matt Jasnosz.

My South African family, for showing me good times and helping me forget the bad: Avril, Belinda, Keith, Bernie, Maxie, Kim, Stacey, Nicole, Chad, Terri, Charlene, Cindy, Marlin, Shanni, and all the little ones.

Sarah Labrie, Andrew Shield, Madeleine Lipshie-Williams, Will Bowling, Fouzia Najar, and Brie Coellner.

Thank you to the incredible staff at the Hospital of the University of Pennsylvania, Perelman Center for Advanced Medicine, and Penn Wissahickon Hospice, for treating my family with respect and compassion. To my mother's friends at the School District of Philadelphia, the Alpha Kappa Alpha Sorority, and the South African expat community in Philadelphia: you've helped me more than you'll ever know.

Thank you to the institutions that supported me in the writing of this book: Columbia University, Art Farm in Nebraska and Ed Dadey, the MacDowell Colony, the NEA (#FDT), Dar-Al Ma'Mûn, Bread Loaf, the FAWC, and VONA.

To Brown University for showing me new worlds. Especially Meredith Steinbach and Kelli Auerbach, who gave me writing, and for allowing me to believe I could pull off this crazy dream.

To my teachers: John Edgar Wideman, Paul Beatty, Margo Jefferson, Danzy Senna, Kiese Laymon, Hilton Als, Ben Marcus, and Binnie Kirshenbaum. Paul, I owe you so much. My peers Angela Flournoy, Alexandra Kleeman, and Naomi Jackson for modeling success, humility, and class.

Emily Firetog, for giving me a chance at a time when no one else would, and for your laughter and friendship.

Thank you to *Transition* magazine, for first recognizing my work in your hallowed pages, and for publishing the story that inspired this book.

Jin Auh and Jessica Friedman at the Wylie Agency, for sticking with me. Allison Lorentzen for your incredible vision, and for believing in this weird little book. Diego Núñez, Olivia Taussig, and Theresa Gaffney for your patience and support. Thank you to Nina Subin for your photographic wizardry.

For Robbie Payne, who is reading Malcolm X in heaven. For my teachers at Swarthmore-Rutledge School and Strath Haven: thanks for recognizing my potential and giving me the confidence that's lasted until this day.

To this big, beautiful, fucked-up country, especially my black and brown brothers and sisters: We gon' be alright.